He came out of the woods…with a baby on his back!

Shauna "Storm" Taylor couldn't believe her eyes. Peeking over the stranger's broad shoulders was a baby! A baby! With one tuft of shiny black hair sticking straight out of its head, and with black button eyes and fat red cheeks.

"Are you lost?" Her eyes drifted to the baby. It was pounding one chubby fist against the man's shoulder. She hoped he was lost. That his presence on her land was uncomplicated——that he had become separated from his wife on a Sunday hike.

But he did not seem to be the kind of man who would get lost. Or be on a family hike, either.

"I need a place to stay," he said, his voice deep and raw as silk.

She stared at him.

A man by himself she could say no to, easily, firmly.

But a man with a baby?

Dear Reader,

The year 2000 marks the twentieth anniversary of Silhouette Books! Ever since May 1980, Silhouette Books—and its flagship line, Silhouette Romance—has published the best in contemporary category romance fiction. And the year's stellar lineups across *all* Silhouette series continue that tradition.

This month in Silhouette Romance, Susan Meier unveils her miniseries BREWSTER BABY BOOM, in which three brothers confront instant fatherhood after inheriting six-month-old triplets! First up is *The Baby Bequest*, in which Evan Brewster does diaper duty…and learns a thing or two about love from his much-younger, mommy-in-the-making assistant. In Teresa Southwick's charming new Silhouette Romance novel, a tall, dark and handsome man decides to woo a jaded nurse *With a Little T.L.C. The Sheik's Solution* is a green-card marriage to his efficient secretary in this lavish fairy tale from Barbara McMahon.

Elizabeth Harbison's CINDERELLA BRIDES series continues with the magnificent *Annie and the Prince*. In Cara Colter's dramatic *A Babe in the Woods*, a mystery man arrives on a reclusive woman's doorstep with a babe on his back—and a gun in his backpack! Then we have a man without a memory who returns to his *Prim, Proper… Pregnant* former fiancée—this unique story by Alice Sharpe is a must-read for those who love twists and turns.

In coming months, look for special titles by longtime favorites Diana Palmer, Joan Hohl, Kasey Michaels, Dixie Browning, Phyllis Halldorson and Tracy Sinclair, as well as many newer but equally loved authors. It's an exciting year for Silhouette Books, and we invite you to join the celebration!

Happy reading!

Mary-Theresa Hussey

Mary-Theresa Hussey
Senior Editor

Please address questions and book requests to:
Silhouette Reader Service
U.S.: 3010 Walden Ave., P.O. Box 1325, Buffalo, NY 14269
Canadian: P.O. Box 609, Fort Erie, Ont. L2A 5X3

A BABE IN THE WOODS

Cara Colter

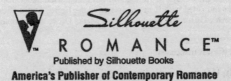

Silhouette

ROMANCE™

Published by Silhouette Books

America's Publisher of Contemporary Romance

To my daughter, Cassidy, with love

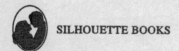 SILHOUETTE BOOKS

ISBN 0-373-19424-2

A BABE IN THE WOODS

Copyright © 2000 by Cara Colter

This edition published by arrangement with Harlequin Books S.A.

® and TM are trademarks of Harlequin Books S.A., used under license.
Trademarks indicated with ® are registered in the United States Patent
and Trademark Office, the Canadian Trade Marks Office and in other
countries.

Visit us at www.romance.net

Printed in U.S.A.

Books by Cara Colter

Silhouette Romance

Dare To Dream #491
Baby in Blue #1161
Husband in Red #1243
The Cowboy, the Baby and the Bride-to-Be #1319
Truly Daddy #1363
A Bride Worth Waiting For #1388
Weddings Do Come True #1406
A Babe in the Woods #1424

CARA COLTER

shares ten acres in the wild Kootenay region of British Columbia with the man of her dreams, three children, two horses, a cat with no tail and a golden retriever who answers best to "bad dog." She loves reading, writing and the woods in winter (no bears). She says life's delights include an automatic garage door opener and the skylight over the bed that allows her to see the stars at night.

She also says, "I have not lived a neat and tidy life, and used to envy those who did. Now I see my struggles as having given me a deep appreciation of life, and of love, that I hope I succeed in passing on through the stories that I tell."

IT'S OUR 20th ANNIVERSARY!
We'll be celebrating all year, starting with these fabulous titles, on sale in January 2000.

Special Edition

#1297 Matt Caldwell: Texas Tycoon
Diana Palmer

#1298 Their Little Princess
Susan Mallery

#1299 The Baby Legacy
Pamela Toth

#1300 Summer Hawk
Peggy Webb

#1301 Daddy by Surprise
Pat Warren

#1302 Lonesome No More
Jean Brashear

Intimate Moments

#979 Murdock's Last Stand
Beverly Barton

#980 Marrying Mike... Again
Alicia Scott

#981 A Drive-By Wedding
Terese Ramin

#982 Midnight Promises
Eileen Wilks

#983 The Comeback of Con MacNeill
Virginia Kantra

#984 Witness... and Wife?
Kate Stevenson

Romance

#1420 The Baby Bequest
Susan Meier

#1421 With a Little T.L.C.
Teresa Southwick

#1422 The Sheik's Solution
Barbara McMahon

#1423 Annie and the Prince
Elizabeth Harbison

#1424 A Babe in the Woods
Cara Colter

#1425 Prim, Proper... Pregnant
Alice Sharpe

Desire

#1267 Her Forever Man
Leanne Banks

#1268 The Pregnant Princess
Anne Marie Winston

#1269 Dr. Mommy
Elizabeth Bevarly

#1270 Hard Lovin' Man
Peggy Moreland

#1271 The Cowboy Takes a Bride
Cathleen Galitz

#1272 Skyler Hawk: Lone Brave
Sheri WhiteFeather

Chapter One

She was being watched. She knew it.

She continued to rock the chair, gently, almost lazily, pushing against the weathered grain of the porch floor with one foot. Waiting. She wasn't really worried. Not yet. The old pump-action shotgun resting outside the cabin door, an arm's length away, gave her a sense of security.

It was probably an animal.

She was accustomed to this sensation. Of thinking she was alone, in the bush, a million miles from the nearest human being, when suddenly she would feel it. Watched. Sometimes she would catch a glimpse of the woodland spy—the flick of a deer's tail, the back end of a bear going the other way—but usually she did not.

A horse, probably Sam, neighed noisily from the corral behind the cabin, a comforting sound. Save for the cheerful bickering of the birds in the forest that ringed the small clearing, it was quiet. A little breeze,

fresh and cold coming off the mountains, teased the
tendrils of dark hair that had fallen out of her braid.
Shoots of tender green grass were beginning to poke
up and she almost imagined she could smell spring.
Everything was normal.

But she did not relax and the sensation of being
watched did not go away. When the hackles rose suddenly on the back of her neck, she knew intuitively
it was not an animal out there watching. Slowly, she
stretched her hands over her head and then flung them
wide, straight out from her shoulders. Her fingertips
touched the shotgun. Straining slightly, her hand
closed around it, drew it close. She pulled it onto her
lap and rocked.

"Might as well come out," she called. "I know
you're there."

Silence.

Shauna Taylor, nicknamed Storm by her brothers,
had arrived at the cabin, accessible only by horseback
or by foot, a short while ago. She had not even emptied her pack boxes yet, had opted instead for a quiet
moment on the porch as evening fell. She cast her
mind back along the trail trying to think if anything
had been unusual, out of place. But there had been
nothing, save for the number of trees down on the
trail after last year's heavy winter. It had taken her a
long time to clear them, and she was small to be handling a chain saw. Jake, her oldest brother, had told
her to wait a week, and he would come with her and
handle the heavy work.

But she knew ranch work, and he would still be
calving in a week. And besides, she was not one to
wait. And certainly not one to let a man do anything
for her that she could do for herself. Even her brother.

Still, her independence was costing her now.

Her muscles ached with fatigue.

That was probably all that was wrong. She was tired. Exhausted. To the point of imagining things.

She scanned the clearing in front of her. She had given the cabin a name in a moment's whimsy. Heart's Rest. Last year she had burned the name onto a wooden sign that was nailed to a towering lodgepole pine just beyond the stone fire pit and the scraggly, rock-lined bed where she had planted wildflowers. Purple mountain saxifrage. Fairy slipper. Fireweed. Indian paintbrush.

Contentment crept up on her, and her fingers relaxed slightly on the shotgun. She was probably imagining things.

She hoped she was.

Still, her other brother, Evan, was fond of telling her she had the most highly developed sense of intuition of anyone he had ever met.

It came, she supposed, from spending so much time alone, loving the solitude of these high and lonesome places. It came from spending more time with horses than people, and the language of her equine friends was the one of intuition, not words.

It came, she supposed, from growing up in the care of her two brothers, far older than she, on a remote ranch in the Coast Mountains west of Williams Lake, British Columbia. Hopelessly unqualified to raise a small girl after their parents had died in a cabin fire, Jake and Evan had unintentionally let her run wild. She knew the forests and mountains around their ranch as well as she knew her own face in the mirror.

She felt safe in these wild places, connected in some way to the immense creative forces of the universe; looked after. Even now, with something out there, she felt confident. This was her turf, and she could handle whatever came her way.

The only time in her life she hadn't felt safe was when she had gone to the University of Alberta in Edmonton for two years. Her brothers, surprisingly resolute, had told her it was okay with them if she became a rancher *someday,* but first they wanted her to know a bigger world. And, truth be told, Storm had felt a strange and tingling eagerness to know a larger world, too.

But the city had been a shock—dodging cars, having to worry about walking alone at night, locking doors.

It was no way to live.

A twig snapped.

She pumped a shell into the shotgun chamber. There were really no places left where a person could be absolutely alone. Hunters and hikers found their way to these isolated spaces. And it didn't bother her.

Unless they tried to be sneaky about it.

Sneakiness bothered her. A lot. Her intuition had failed her once, back there in Edmonton. When she'd been fooled by a too-handsome face and a smooth way.

She wondered if her brothers would have laughed, seeing their tomboy sister experimenting with makeup. She'd even bought a skirt, ridiculously short, now that she thought about it. Dorian's eyes widening with appreciation had made that little scrap of material worth its enormous price.

Storm curtly turned the memory off and listened. She told herself to smarten up. It wouldn't really be fair if she took a shot at some unsuspecting hiker because she detested sneakiness.

The truth was she would have dearly liked to pump a few rounds into the air around Dorian, just to scare the living daylights out of him. Once she'd found out the truth.

Married.

The snake had been married.

If she was alone up here at her mountain retreat, it didn't matter. And if she wasn't, it wouldn't hurt to show she knew how to handle the gun and was not afraid to use it.

Boom! *Take that, Dorian.*

She shot high, into the air. The sound of the shotgun blast echoed over the quiet clearing. Casually, she pumped another shell into the chamber. At first she thought she had failed to flush out whatever kind of varmint hid in the trees.

And then a thin and reedy wail flowed into the silence left by the blast of the shotgun. Storm's mouth fell open and she leaped to her feet. She set the shotgun down and raced down the cabin's crumbling stone steps and across the clearing toward the sound.

Because there was really no mistaking that sound.

Even for a woman like her who refused to even hold one.

There was a baby in those woods.

A man slipped out of the trees before she was halfway across the clearing.

Storm skidded to a halt.

He was an imposing man, maybe two inches over six feet. He was incredibly broad across his shoulders and through his chest, and that broadness narrowed dramatically at his flat belly. His legs were long and lean, the clean line of hard muscle evident through the fabric of heavy denim. His khaki-colored shirt-sleeves were rolled up, revealing a naked length of very powerful forearm. The first few buttons of his shirt were open, showing a tangle of dark, curling chest hair.

He carried himself with confidence, loose-limbed and yet *ready*. Ready for anything. A man who could deal with the elements, and not just survive but be made stronger by them, even more able to face the challenges of a world as wild and rugged as he was.

Her gaze went to his face. It was a face of raw, rugged and uncompromising strength. His cheekbones were high, his nose straight, his jaw square. He had the faintest hint of a cleft in his chin. He could have been utterly gorgeous if not for a hardness that lingered in the turn of his mouth. His hair was neat and short, but sweat-darkened, and she suspected it was a shade lighter than the dark chocolate it looked to be. His skin had the weathered look of a man who spent a great deal of time outdoors, and the coppery tones of it made the gray of his eyes seem deep and cool, like the gray of icy mountain creeks.

His eyes were watchful, wary and weary.

Beyond weary. The man was exhausted.

Then a movement over his left shoulder drew her gaze from his. She could feel her eyes widen and her mouth drop open.

Peeking over his shoulder was a baby. A baby! With one tuft of shiny black hair sticking straight out from its head, and with black button eyes and fat red cheeks with grimy tear stains running down them.

"Are you alone?" the man asked.

The exhaustion she saw in his eyes was echoed in that voice—a deep voice, raw as silk.

Still, it was not a good question to be asked by a complete stranger. A man who had watched for a long time before he had made his presence known. Who might never have made his presence known if she had not flushed him out with a shotgun blast. The question was not asked out of any kind of friendliness.

"No," she lied, instinctively, "I'm not alone."

Some tension leaped in him, coiled along his muscles. A man ready for anything, including a fight. *With a baby on his back.*

"Who's with you?" he asked, his eyes scanning the cabin behind her.

"None of your business."

"Who's with you?" he asked again, quietly, but with some unmistakable iron in his voice.

"My friend Sam," she said defiantly. A nice name. Sturdy sounding. Strong. Loyal. Which is why she had given it to the big bay gelding she used for her saddle horse.

"Why didn't Sam come out when you fired off that shotgun?" he asked. Something in him relaxed. The faintest hint of amusement lit those eyes before the weariness and caution drowned it.

"Why didn't you?" she snapped back.

"I thought you might shoot me."

"I still might."

"You're not a very neighborly kind of person," he pointed out, mildly.

"Me and Sam aren't much used to neighbors."

"But you're used to shotguns." Something, not quite a smile, lifted a corner of that firm mouth. "You and *Sam.*"

He had obviously figured out Sam was fiction, but she tried again, anyway. "That's why he didn't come out. He's used to me blasting off that old shotgun at varmints."

The stranger's smile, thankfully, died before it was ever completely born, and cool eyes scanned her face, then the clearing and then the cabin, before returning to her. "You're alone," he decided.

She wanted to insist she wasn't, but knew it was pointless. She suspected this man's intuition was as fine-honed as her own was. Maybe more so. Despite the weariness, there was an alertness about him that reminded her of wild animals poised on the edge of danger, getting ready to flee. Or fight.

He's in trouble, Storm thought, bad trouble.

She wondered why she did not sense imminent danger, then realized that her intuition had been known to let her down in this one critical area. Men.

"Are you lost?" Her eyes drifted to the baby. It was pounding one chubby fist against the man's shoulder and had another tangled in the dark silk of his hair. A lesser man might have winced or tried to unlock the baby's determined grip, but his attention remained totally focused on her. As if she might make a dash for that shotgun. People who were lost were usually not quite so on guard.

Still, she wished he was lost. That his presence here was uncomplicated—that he had become separated from his wife on a Sunday hike.

But he did not seem to be the kind of man who would get lost. Or be on a family hike, either. Her eyes went to that telltale finger. No gold band. And no little white line where one might have been a short while ago. She considered herself a quick learner.

"I need a place to stay."

She stared at him.

"I was up here years ago. I remembered the cabin."

He could be anybody. He'd probably kidnapped that baby. He didn't look like the kind of man who would find taking a baby on a hiking trip a whole lot of fun.

"A place to stay? *Here?*"

"Only for a couple of days."

Oh, great. Now he was appealing to her softer side. A man by himself, she could say no to easily, firmly. But a man with a baby?

He pitched forward a step, and she saw with sudden horror that there was a small pool of blood where he had stood before.

"You're hurt!"

"It's just a scratch."

She could see a red stain now spreading around the side of his shirt, just above the waistline of his jeans, from his back.

She went forward. Suddenly she didn't have to think at all. She went behind him. She could tell he didn't like that one little bit. Like an old-time gunslinger, he didn't like having his back exposed.

The baby was in the top part of a backpack not designed for babies. Bungee straps secured the unusual cargo. She stretched up, unstrapped the cords deftly and took the wriggling little bundle down. If she was taller, she might have been able to see what else was in the pack, and it might have answered some questions for her. But she was not taller, and the next five seconds did not hold much promise of her growing.

The man smelled faintly of soap, overlaid with woodsy aromas of sunshine and sweat. And blood. She glanced down and saw the dark-red stain just above his right hip.

She hoped to hell he wasn't gun shot. They were a hard ride from the trailhead and a half hour to the tiny hamlet of Thunder Lake after that, if she could get her cranky truck to start right away.

Why did she think he had been shot?

He could have caught himself on a branch. Or fallen on a rock.

The baby gurgled at her and tried to insert pudgy fingers in her nose. It diverted her attention from the man's presence, though even not looking at him, she could *feel* him. It was as if electricity hummed and hissed in the air around him, and made her quiet clearing vibrate with tension.

The baby's weight was solid in her arms. She didn't think she'd held a baby before. A baby was a rare commodity in a town like Thunder Lake. When there was one around, a baby, Storm avoided the ruckus. And now she knew why. It made a person kind of go all soft and mushy inside, even when a man was dripping blood all over her yard.

"Come on," she said, lugging the baby up the stairs. Her mind raced. An injured man and a baby had just showed up at her cabin. He was relieved that no one was here but her, a woman on her own. Maybe she was the one with trouble. Bad trouble. She ducked a little pink finger aimed at her eye. The baby clouded things. It was hard to consider the possibility of menace in the merry presence of the child.

The man paused behind her on the porch. She

glanced over her shoulder to see him unloading the shotgun. He slipped the shell into his pocket.

There's plenty more where that one came from, buster.

The cabin was small and cozy inside. A primitive wooden table stood at its center, and a potbellied wood burner was in the corner. Two sets of rough open cupboards were on either side of a sink with a hand pump for a faucet. There was one tiny window, and in a rare fit of domesticity Storm had nailed up two squares of checkered red fabric that passed for curtains if they weren't inspected too closely.

Her visitor went and pulled back the matching curtains that separated the bunk beds from the main cabin area. When his inspection proved they were alone, the last of the tension relaxed out of those hard muscles. He turned to face her.

"This has changed. You can sleep a crowd in here now," he commented of the six bunks. "How come?"

"It's an army training center. I'm expecting the troops at any moment."

"Led by Sam?" he asked dryly, slipping his arms from the backpack straps and letting it slide to the floor, taking in the rest of the cabin in a glance.

His gaze rested for a moment on the early-blooming wildflowers she had stuck in a tin at the center of the table when she'd first arrived. Now she was sorry she had done that. She thought it made her look somewhat vulnerable, which was not the appearance she wanted to give right at the moment.

"I better have a look at that wound," she said.

"It doesn't qualify as a wound."

"Well, whatever it qualifies as, you're dripping

blood on my floor, so sit down." She shoved a chair back for him with her foot.

He looked narrowly at her, unaccustomed to taking orders, though she suspected he may have given a few in his day. His compliance was reluctant. He winced when he sat down.

He picked up a brochure on her table, and she resisted an urge to snatch it from his hand, to keep her secrets, while she probed his.

"Storm Mountain Trail Rides," he read out loud. "Come and see the beauty and panorama of Canada's great north by horseback. Day, overnight or weekly excursions. Limited to five riders. Mid-June to mid-September." His eyes flicked to the bunks, counting, and then went back to the brochure. "Led by fully qualified guide Storm Taylor. What the hell kind of name is that?" he muttered. "Storm?"

"I'll have a look at that wound now."

But he wasn't done with the brochure. He flipped it over, and there was her picture with her name under it.

"So," he said, "Storm of Storm Mountain, you're getting ready for your trail-riding season to open. No guests booked, for what, three weeks?"

"You're getting blood on my chair," she pointed out. "I think we'd better take care of that."

The baby made a sound somewhere between a mew and a squeak.

"I think he's hungry," he said.

His concern for the baby's well-being was somewhat reassuring. Storm held the baby at arms' length. *He.* His lashes were thick and sooty as a chimney brush. He waved his chubby arms and legs at her and gurgled. He was wearing plain blue terry-cloth pajamas with feet in them. He seemed content, like a baby who could wait while she saw to a man bleeding all over her furnishings, humble as they might be. She considered where to set him. The counter or tabletop seemed like a good idea, but given his roly-poly build he might roll off like a live beach ball. Instead she plopped him down on his padded fanny on the floor.

He flopped forward at the waist and grabbed at a dust mote.

"Does he crawl?" she asked dubiously.

The man gave the baby a measuring look. "No."

But Storm felt he was guessing. He didn't know if the baby crawled. She had the awful feeling he didn't know much more about that baby than she did.

Well, maybe a little more. He knew the baby was male.

The baby captured the dust mote and after trying to put it in his ear and his eye, he finally managed to cram his prize into his mouth.

Storm leaped forward and dug it out. The baby chomped happily on her fingers with his toothless gums. It should have been utterly disgusting, but for some reason it wasn't so bad. Casting one more look at the man at the table, she went and scooped her bedroll off one of the bunks, unrolled it and put the baby on it. She hoped his diaper wouldn't spring a leak on her only bedding.

The baby flopped over even further, until his nose was practically touching the sleeping bag, and then with a mighty grunt, pushed his legs out behind him, so now he was lying on his stomach. He flailed away, grunting with exertion.

Storm watched for a moment, fascinated, then turned to the man at her kitchen table.

"Take off your shirt."

"I hardly know you." That hint of a smile again.

She wondered if he used that smile to disarm people, because there was no answering warmth in his gray eyes, only watchfulness, appraisal. He was measuring her every move.

I'm in trouble, she thought, but kept her voice steady. "And that's how it's going to stay," she said firmly. "Take off your shirt."

He pulled his shirt tails out of the waistband of his pants, flinching when the fabric pulled at the clotted blood at his side. He unbuttoned, revealing to her slowly the broad swell of his chest, the rock-hard cut of pectoral muscles. He slid the shirt off, and she had to bite her tongue to keep from gasping at the absolute male perfection of him. His skin was bronze and silky over sinewy muscles. Hair curled, thick and springy, over the broad, hard plain of his chest. The hair narrowed down to a taut stomach, then disappeared inside the waistband of his jeans.

She turned abruptly. What was wrong with her? This man had arrived on her mountain and at her cabin with an attitude that aroused all her suspicions. She needed to keep her mind crystal clear so that she knew how to deal with this troubling situation. Patch him up and send him on his way, or patch him up and be on her way? What was not going to happen, what was not even a possibility, was sharing her cabin with him for a few days.

Not that he had to know that just yet.

On the top shelf of one of her open cupboards was a first-aid kit, and she took it down and sorted carefully through the bandages, painkillers and swabs.

When she turned back to him, she saw that he had

straddled the chair so she could get a better look at his wound. His broad and naked back was enough to cloud anyone's thinking! Again, she was taken by the color of his skin. Bronze. It made it look warm and silky, skin that invited touching.

She bent quickly and looked at where the blood blossomed like an obscene crimson flower slightly above and to the side of his hip. When she cleaned away the blood, it really did look like a scratch, a mean scratch though, deep, wide and ragged.

"How did you do this?"

"I was trying to chop my way through a mess of brush. The ax swung back and clipped me."

She studied the wound, thinking it was at least possible, though the wound seemed to be in an odd place and the edges of it not clean enough to have been caused by an ax. She continued to suspect the wound was the result of a gunshot, though if it was a gunshot it was superficial, a graze. Her brothers would say she read too many suspense novels.

"Which way did you come in from?" she asked, striving to sound casual.

He hesitated. "From the east."

"That's a tough way to come in." She didn't say a weird way. He had come cross-country, from a little-known logging road. It explained why she had seen no sign of him on her trail.

Doing her best not to hurt him more, she finished cleaning around the wound. His skin felt exactly the way she had known it would feel—like warm silk wrapped over steel.

She continued to probe, trying to keep her questions conversational and casual. "What would make you come here? With a baby?"

"We're on vacation."

"A vacation?" Too late, she tried to snatch back the skepticism out of her tone.

He shrugged, and she glanced up from her swabbing of that cut, to see his eyes on her, hooded, measuring.

She turned hastily from him to her humble kitchen counter and mixed up Jake's favorite old family formula to put on the injury.

"This place doesn't seem like it would be first choice for someone with a baby to take a holiday," she ventured, glancing back at him.

"Really?" he said evenly. "Fresh air. Great fishing. What is that?"

"Turpentine and brown sugar. It kills infection."

"No kidding?" he growled.

"Kerosene oil works, too, but you have to be careful with it. It'll blister the skin."

"Really?"

"And a bit of chimney soot and lard will work, but it's messy." She offered these folksy little gems to him partly to take his mind off the pain, partly to make him think she was just a naive mountain girl, not sophisticated enough to be even contemplating the possibility he might have kidnapped that baby.

"My brother Jake would have put a spiderweb on to stop the bleeding, but I'll just use one of these regular bandages."

"Shortage of spiderwebs?"

"I think the baby is eating them."

He chuckled at that, a reluctant and dry sound deep in his throat.

She unrolled medical gauze around his entire lower body, back to belly, to hold the bandage in place and keep pressure on it. It was amazingly hard not to touch a man while doing that, so she simply surrendered to the circumstances.

A mistake. Every time her hands grazed his skin, his muscles, physical sensation rocked through her. She had never been struck by lightning, thank God, but she was pretty sure it would feel just about like this. She felt a need so naked and demanding it set her teeth on edge. Where had it come from? This sudden need that felt greater than a need for food or water. To be kissed hard and held soft.

Not by this man!

A stranger, with a suspicious wound, and a baby she did not think was his.

The air around him practically tingled with danger, mystery and an aura of exotic worlds she knew nothing about.

She had a lot of questions to ask and she ordered them in her mind as she bent to the task at hand, knowing, even before she asked, that his answers would not satisfy her curiosity, nor lessen the sense of danger vibrating off him in waves that were unmistakably sensuous.

"You're trussing me up like a mummy," he complained.

"Since you mention it, where is junior's mommy?"

"She died. She died when he was born."

"And you're his daddy, right?"

A flick of emotion in those complicated eyes. "Right."

She felt a shiver go up and down her spine as she registered the lie, but she said with absolute calm, "Well, you're welcome to the cabin. It's primitive but if it's fresh air and fishing you're looking for, you'll find plenty of both here. I have to move on, but if you need me to leave you anything—''

"You can't go anywhere tonight. It's nearly dark.''

It was said pleasantly enough, but she had the uneasy feeling she had just become a prisoner. Still, she had her shotgun outside the door, and her wits.

"That's probably a good idea," she said pleasantly. "It wouldn't be smart to go thrashing around the mountains in the dark. We'll muddle through tonight, and I'll go in the morning.''

She cast him a look from under her lashes. She knew these mountain trails, night or day. And besides, there would be a moon.

Ben McKinnon watched his prisoner carefully. Because that was what she was now. He could not risk letting her go and telling anyone she had seen him with the baby. He wondered if she knew it, and suspected she did. Her eyes, gorgeous blue, almost turquoise, sparkled with spirit and intelligence, despite the folksy cobwebs and chimney soot routine.

She was a complication he didn't need. One he resented. He had not planned on anyone being at the cabin. He needed five days, maybe six, in a place where he could not be found and would not be looked for. Meanwhile, Jack Day, a friend from the Federal Intelligence Agency, would find out who had betrayed him and if the vengeance of Noel East's political enemies extended to the baby. Back there in the woods, Ben had ditched a high-tech two-way radio that he could check in on later.

Noel East. A humble and courageous man, a single

father, who had put his name forward as a candidate in the tiny country of Crescada's first free elections.

Ben had been assigned to protect him. The immensity of his failure would haunt him into old age.

The baby began to howl, thankfully, bringing him back to the here and now before he saw again in his mind's eye that strangely peaceful look on Noel's face, heard again his dying words.

"How can something so small make so much noise?" the woman asked, astounded.

"I've been asking myself the same thing for three days," he said, and saw his mistake register in her face. He'd just said he was the kid's father, one of those lies he had become adept at telling in the course of his work. Necessary lies. "He's hungry," he said, hoping that interpreting the caterwauling would win him back some lost ground.

"Have you got food for him?"

"In the pack." He sprang up when she moved toward it, intercepting her smoothly. "I'll get it."

He seemed to be doing very poorly here. He had failed to allay her suspicions, failed to convince her he was the baby's father, now she knew there was something in that pack he didn't want her to see.

"We need to heat this stuff up," he said, again hoping to impress her with what an expert he was on formula preparation.

"I'll get some wood and we'll light the stove."

As soon as she was out the door, Ben set down the formula. He shut his eyes and pressed a hand against his wound. Hell, he hadn't hurt like this for a long time. But turpentine and brown sugar?

He limped over to the small window and looked out into the gathering darkness. She was splitting kindling, not heading for the horses. He could hear her whistling, which he thought was probably a ploy to make him think she was more accepting of this situation than she was.

"Would you give it a rest?" he asked the baby.

The baby ignored him.

He was not a man used to being ignored. Or used to babies. And certainly not used to a woman like that. When he'd first seen her on the porch, he'd thought she was a boy. Then she had stretched, and not only shown him some very unboyish curves but her face had come out from under the shadow of the brim of her hat, and her thick dark braid had flopped over her slender shoulder. She was more than lovely. Striking. Stunning.

What was a woman like that doing running a rugged business like this by herself? Hiding, he figured, probably every bit as much as he was. Just from something different.

He was willing to bet, from the suspicion in her eyes, it had been a man.

He resented that unknown man, too. Destroying her trust when he needed a trusting woman most.

Giving her one more glance, he went back to his pack and found a little plastic container of green powder that claimed it became peas when water was added. He dumped some into a dish and added water. Instant pond scum.

The baby stopped crying as soon as he picked him up, a reaction that pleased and horrified him at the same time.

"Open up," he muttered.

The baby opened his mouth, then closed it firmly

just before the spoon made it in. Green stuff dribbled down his little blue outfit.

Ben scowled. The baby pouted. Ben glanced around. He listened. He could still hear the ax biting into wood.

"Okay, okay. Chugga-chugga choo-choo. Here comes the train. Open the tunnel. Open the tunnel!"

The baby laughed, the tunnel opened, the green slime went in, was chewed thoughtfully and swallowed. He held out the spoon again. The baby pouted. The kid wouldn't eat now without the train routine.

Ben felt he had been through just about the toughest week in his career, first losing Noel East, who had become his friend, and then smuggling this baby, Noel's child, out of Crescada. And now he had to play choo-choo to get the damn kid to eat? It didn't seem that life could get much more unfair.

The baby got a look of intense concentration on his face. He turned a most unbecoming shade of purple. A horrible aroma drifted up to Ben's nostrils.

He conceded his fate; it could get more unfair after all.

Chapter Two

Storm felt perspiration popping out on her forehead.

"Give," her unexpected guest told her quietly. "You can't win. You're going to break your arm trying."

Storm braced her elbow, closed her eyes, tightened her grip on his hand and pushed with everything she had.

Damn. He was holding her. Toying with her. She suspected he could put her down in a second if he chose.

They were arm wrestling over who was going to look after that diaper. Jake and Evan had been arm wrestling with her since she was a tot. They'd shown her a trick, a way to snap her wrist quickly at the very onset of the match, which gave her pretty even odds against superior strength.

And it often told her a great deal about a man, the way he accepted his defeat or his victory. And she *needed* to know something about this man.

She had never arm wrestled Dorian. A mistake. She probably could have saved herself a great deal of heartache if she'd used her regular measuring stick of character, instead of pretending to be something she was not. She nearly shuddered at the thought of that bright-red lipstick and thick black mascara that she'd hidden behind.

Still, it seemed to have been a terrible mistake to suggest an arm wrestle to this man, too.

Because when his hand had locked around hers, she had felt the strength in it. A pure strength. And she had felt something else.

Pure sizzle.

Right down to the bottom of her belly.

She'd arm wrestled just about every man in Thunder Lake and never, ever felt that sudden "woomph" deep in her stomach.

She glanced into the clear gray of his eyes and felt it again. A pull to him that was unfathomable given their circumstances, given the fact he thought he could make her stay here, and she planned to prove him wrong.

She told herself, sternly, she only *needed* to know something of him so she knew what to do once she had left here. Give him a few days with the baby to have his vacation? Or go down that mountain as fast as she could and come back with the law?

The very fact that she did not feel free to leave when she wanted should be telling her exactly what she needed to know.

But her intuition was placing her in a position of inner turmoil. Her intuition looked into the clearness of his eyes and saw, lurking just beneath the cool, still surface, strength of spirit.

The facts spoke of something else. The wound, his presence at her cabin not really explained, the baby most likely not his. He wasn't even comfortable changing a diaper!

Childishly, she decided how the arm-wrestling match finished would make her decision for her. If he won, she would go down the mountain and forget she had ever seen him or that baby. If she won, she was coming back with Constable Jennings from the Royal Canadian Mounted Police.

She closed her eyes again, focused all her strength, felt her arm begin to tremble with effort and exertion. And nearly fell off her chair when he suddenly released her hand.

"Hey!" she said, miffed.

His eyes weren't clear now, but deliberately hooded. "A draw," he said blandly.

"It was not. I was about to take you." She knew darn well the exact opposite was true.

"You were about to break your arm."

"Oh, right."

"I could see the white line of your bone right through your skin. Trust me. It was a draw."

He had called the match because he thought he was going to harm her. That told her a reassuring little fact she needed to know. It would seem he wasn't planning to hurt her. It would seem he was—the word *noble* flitted through her mind. She gave herself a shake.

She got to her feet abruptly, wiping her hand on her jeans as if she could wipe away the sudden feeling that had engulfed her when she had looked into his eyes.

They were the eyes of a dangerous man. Mysterious. Cool. Calm. And yet she could not help but feel the strength in them was linked to her own future.

He nodded at her. "You're very strong."

On the outside. Still, it was a good response. He had won the match, even if he was *noble* enough not to say so. He was sure of himself. He didn't need to overpower her to nurture his own self-esteem. And he didn't rub her face in his superior strength, either.

No surprises there. He oozed that standoffish kind of confidence of a man who walked tall and walked alone.

She spun away from that steady searching look in his eyes and looked at the baby. The aroma wafting off that wee individual was every bit as astonishing as the amount of noise he could make.

Gingerly, she picked up a clean diaper and studied it. "What's his name?" she asked the man behind her.

And then realized she didn't know *his* name either.

"You can call him Rocky. You don't have to change him. I've managed before."

"A deal's a deal. And what can I call you?"

Hesitation. "Ben."

She unfolded the diaper and flipped it trying to figure out which way it went on. What kind of man didn't even want to tell you his name? Perhaps the arm-wrestle test had failed to reveal his character to her after all.

Really, all she had to remember was one thing.

She was a terrible judge of character when it came to men. Arm wrestling or no.

Suddenly, he was right behind her. He had come on leopard-quiet feet, and so she gasped with soft surprise when he reached around her and took the diaper, laid it out flat on the counter and contemplated it for a moment.

His arm was brushing her shoulder.

She could feel the corded muscles in it, the heat coming off it. He smelled of the forest and of man, and compared to the other smell in the cabin it was pretty heady stuff.

She gritted her teeth.

And reminded herself. *His wound was suspicious. She was a terrible judge of men. Whose baby was this, anyway?* She moved slightly so that she was out of range of that muscular arm and his masculine potency.

"Like that," he decided, placing the diaper, and then casually, "And what should I call you?"

"Storm, just like it says on the brochure."

"Storm." He repeated it, looking at her as if he was looking deeper, trying to see beyond what his eyes told him. "A nickname?"

"My brothers always called me that." Her brothers had always said the name accurately reflected her temperament, though she didn't share that with Ben.

He nodded at that, satisfied she suspected that his own assessment of her character, arrived at in less than fifteen minutes, had just been confirmed.

"Well, Storm, I think the moment of truth has arrived."

Great. Just spill the beans.

But that wasn't the truth he was talking about. He scooped the baby off the floor, held him at arm's length for a moment and then laid him on the counter. "Somehow we'll figure this out together. Any suggestions for step one?"

Rocky gurgled and smiled, somehow not in the least intimidated by this intimidating man.

"Very helpful," Ben told the baby, and she detected there might be a sense of humor behind all that steel.

"How about the snaps on the sleeper?" she suggested, trying not to smile, trying to remember her most important step was to get out of here. She could contemplate what step two would be after she had accomplished step one.

"Even better."

She watched his hands, strong and brown, make short work of the snaps. They were not, she decided, hands accustomed to this kind of work, and yet he was not a man who would do anything hesitantly.

Her own shirt, western-style, had snaps on it.

She ordered her mind not to go there.

Ben stripped off the sleeper with the same let's-get-the-job-done efficiency. The baby was pink and dimpled all over. He waved his arms and legs, apparently delighting in the little explosions of odor his every vigorous movement caused.

"Have you got any clothes-pegs?" Ben asked.

Her lifestyle often required drying things on an inside line. She found the tin with the clothespins in it and brought it to him.

She had thought he intended to use them as diaper fasteners, and despite her desire not to let him win her over in any way, she burst out laughing when he carefully put one on the end of his nose.

"Want one?" he asked, his voice only marginally less sexy for the nasal twang in it.

"Does it help?"

"Yeah."

So she nodded and found a clothespin clipped on the end of her nose. She was willing to bet she looked a lot less sexy—not, she realized, that she had looked that sexy to begin with. Not that she even wanted to think about why she might care if she looked sexy or not.

The clothespin helped. It hurt, but it was worth it.

"All right. Flap one, down." He pulled the plastic tab, and the baby's right leg sprang free of the diaper. She listened to his voice and heard a clue there. She would take money that there was something military in his background.

"Flap two, down," he said in that same pilot-preparing-for-takeoff tone. He pulled number two. With lightning speed he had the diaper down and off and had handed her the damp cloth. He was running for the door.

She thought she might embarrass herself by puking, but oddly enough the chore didn't bother her.

In seconds the baby was clean. She looked at the little jar of petroleum jelly, dabbed her fingers in and swabbed a generous amount on the baby's little pink bottom. Ben was back.

"What did you do with that thing?" she asked.

"I put it in your fire pit. It puffed up like a big marshmallow and disappeared."

"Great, do the same with this." She handed him the washcloth.

"Isn't it brand new?"

"I don't care."

He gave her an approving look and went back out. She plopped the baby on the fresh diaper.

"Don't try and do up those tabs with petroleum jelly on your hands," he called over his shoulder.

Too late. "Why not?"

"They won't—"

The grease-slicked tab refused to cling to the diaper. She tried to wipe it off. No dice.

"—stick." He came back in and looked over her shoulder. "Beginner's mistake. But I have a short supply of diapers. I can't throw any of them out."

"You can always use moss," she said.

"Really? And if there's no moss, maybe a spider's web or two?"

"Are you making fun of me?"

"No, ma'am." But he turned quickly from her and began rummaging in the first-aid kit. When he turned back to her, roll of gauze in hand, the glint of amusement that had leaped in his eyes was gone. It was just as well. When these small traces of personality pushed through his surface remoteness, she saw a man who could be altogether too charming.

"I think it's wonderful that the native people knew how to use what was around them—weren't dependent on stores and factories to provide them with something so simple as a diaper," she informed him.

"You won't get any argument from me."

"Good," she said with great dignity.

"Just as long as you don't start mixing up the turpentine and brown sugar as a substitute for baby powder."

She glared at him, reminding herself it was a *good* thing if he thought she was some kind of backwoods bumpkin. The last thing he would be expecting would be a daring, midnight escape. The last laugh would be hers.

The only part that was too bad was that she

wouldn't have the enjoyment of seeing his face when he woke up in the morning to an empty cabin.

He flashed her a grin that nearly stole the breath out of her lungs and then ignored her as he wrapped the gauze around the waistband of the baby's diaper, finally tying it in a neat bow in the front. "How's that for using the resources at hand?"

She tried not to smile, but that ridiculous bow got her. She smiled. And then she laughed.

And so did he.

And she knew three things about him. One, he did not laugh often.

Two. He had removed the clothespin from his nose and she had not. She snatched off the clothespin.

Three. He was a complete novice at changing diapers.

The laughter died in her, and it did in him, too. They regarded each other warily.

"This isn't your baby, is it?" Stupid to ask. She wanted to lull him into a false sense of security, and yet she needed to know. At least that.

He hesitated, shot her a look out of the corner of his eye. His features were suddenly closed. He carefully folded the baby's arms back into the sleeves of his sleeper and tucked his legs back inside the fabric.

"No," he finally said. "He's not my baby."

"Then why do you have him?"

"It's a long story, Storm." His voice was laced with weariness and remoteness.

She ignored the way she felt when he said her name, his voice deep-timbered, as sexy as the touch of hot hands across the back of her neck.

"I seem to have some time on my hands." She folded her arms stubbornly over her chest.

"The less you know the better."

She took in her breath sharply at that, and he watched her narrowly, then looked away, ran a hand through the rich darkness of his hair, sighed and looked back.

"I can tell you this: I've been entrusted with his care. I'm not one of those dads you read about in the paper. Or a kidnapper."

"How long have you had him?"

"A few days."

"Is his name really Rocky?"

Hesitation. "No."

She studied him long and hard. He did not flinch under her scrutiny but met her gaze evenly. Still, there was something hooded in his eyes. A place that was hard and cold, that had seen too much.

Sometimes intuition was a curse.

Because beyond all that she thought she saw a man dying of loneliness.

She reminded herself that a woman could die of perpetual stupidity, too.

"What's his real name?" she asked.

"I can't tell you that."

"Won't."

"All right. Won't."

"And for how long have you been *entrusted* with his care?"

"I don't know yet."

She realized she had better not press him anymore. She did not want to alert him to the fact she could not stay under these circumstances.

Ben discovered he liked looking at her.

Those wide eyes were incredible. He was not sure

he had ever seen human eyes so close to turquoise in shade. They tilted up at the corners. She had taken off the hat, and her hair was dark and shiny like a river of braided black silk. Her features were even and pleasing, a faint scattering of freckles over a pert little nose. Her lips were full and sensuous, and he wondered what it would be like to taste them.

And chastised himself for wondering. He had a job to do: to keep that baby safe until some semblance of sanity returned to Crescada, until whoever had murdered the baby's father, Noel East, was safely in custody, where he could not harm the baby, Rockford. Ben knew his focus had to stay crystal clear, and contemplating the taste of lips would not keep his focus crystal clear.

He forced himself to study her analytically, to figure out if she was going to be an asset or a liability if things went sour.

An asset.

There was strength in her face. Independence. Intelligence.

And she was strong physically, as well.

He had been totally taken by surprise by the power in her arms when she had innocently suggested an arm wrestle. He'd been so taken off guard by the quick and powerful flick of her wrist that had she pressed her advantage she might have taken him before he knew what hit him.

He had better keep that in mind. He needed his guard up or she could take him before he knew what hit him.

The question was, take him where?

A question he really did not want an answer for. At all.

A mystery. She was a mystery. Even her name held some of her mystery, something brewing within her that was elemental and fierce, a force of nature that a man would be foolish to underestimate.

In his experience women who looked like her walked the runways of the world. What was she doing running a string of horses, alone, in this remote and beautiful north country?

Why had she challenged him to an arm wrestle, when she could have gotten him to do anything she wanted, up to and including handling that disgusting diaper all by himself, with a bat of her gorgeous tangled lashes?

One thing his life did not need was any more intrigue.

His whole life had been intrigue. Dark secrets. Danger. He'd been recruited to do federal intelligence work at age twenty-one. He had thought he was embarking on a career of high romance and adventure.

Instead the road had been a lonely one that had turned him hard and cold. Much too hard and cold to be entrusted with something so fragile as a baby.

Or this woman.

Still, here he was, and if there was one thing he had learned—and learned swiftly—it was that it was very rare for a man in his line of work to ever be handed circumstances that were to his liking. He learned to make do with what he was dealt.

This time the cards had turned up a baby whose family was dead and who needed his protection. And a woman with far too many questions making her eyes burn brilliant.

He spent ten years living by the military adage, "Need to know." What you didn't need to know, you weren't told. And what others didn't need to know, you didn't tell them.

And this woman in front of him wanted to know everything. For her own safety, and that of the baby, he would tell her nothing for as long as he could.

Oddly, the way her eyes were resting on him, he suspected she already knew things about him that he did not know about himself.

And it scared the living daylights out of him.

He thrust the baby at her. "Maybe you could try and shovel some of that green stuff into him."

She looked awkward with the baby, and yet her face softened with tenderness when she looked at him.

And for a blinding moment a renegade yearning shot out from under the steel trap of Ben's hard-earned control—a yearning to walk away from this life of loneliness and be a part of a circle of love.

It occurred to him he'd given Storm his real name, evidence that his thinking was already being clouded by her presence, by that restlessness within himself that had made him take the job with Rocky's father on pure whimsy, instead of reason. He'd liked the man. And look where that had gotten him. He should know by now that forming attachments was something he should guard against.

Cursing inwardly, he turned away from her and the baby and went outside.

He listened. The forest was dark and silent. He listened inside himself. His heart told him he had not been followed. And that he was in danger of a different kind.

A kind he had never faced before, and was not trained to defend against.

* * *

Storm spooned the green stuff into Rocky, who slurped it back with relish. He waved his hands wildly in the air in between bites.

Ben had gone outside. She was glad. His presence did things to her. Made her aware of something deep, dark and dangerous inside herself.

Something that had never been tapped or touched.

Not even by her infatuation with Dorian.

The baby finished eating, and she dampened a cloth and wiped his face. She took him and rested his head against her shoulder and rocked him, and he went to sleep almost instantly. She liked the puddled warmth of him in her arms. Only after he had started to feel heavy did she lay him carefully back on the sleeping bag on the floor.

The night was turning chilly as it would do in the mountains in the spring, and even in the summer.

Ben came back in, the load of firewood he carried effortlessly showing the corded muscles of his arms to distinct advantage. "It's cold out," he said briefly.

He put down the wood carefully, so as not to wake the baby, then went and gazed down at him for a moment, unaware of how his hard features softened with momentary tenderness.

And certainly unaware of what that softening of those features did to her.

Filled her with something.

Yearning.

"I guess we should eat," she said abruptly. "I've got plenty of grub in my pack boxes. I'll go get them."

She didn't know if he accompanied her out of a sense of chivalry or because he was guarding her, but they went together to where she had left the pack boxes by the corral. He went unhesitatingly and held out his hand to her old horse.

"That's Sam," she said, disarmed by the look on his face. What was it? Wistfulness?

He turned and gave her a look, the wistfulness replaced by a look of dry amusement. "So this is Sam."

She shrugged, watching how he stroked the horse's forehead, scratched along his mane. "You like horses," she said. "You've been around them a bit, too."

"We used to raise quarter horses when I was a kid. I grew up on a ranch in Wyoming."

"I should have known."

"What?"

"Cowboy. You can take off the boots and the hats, and you can put years between you and the range, but it's still there."

"What's still there?"

She was sorry she had blurted out the thought, sorrier still he was pursuing it into her private thoughts about him. "Arrogance," she said. But she thought *mystique, strength, self-reliance. The way they held themselves. The pride in their eyes.*

A slight frown creased his forehead. "You're an expert on cowboys?"

"I was raised by two of them."

"I should have known."

"What?"

"Cowgirl."

"And you're an expert on cowgirls?"

"No. We were pretty isolated where we were. I

don't know the first thing about cowgirls. But if I had to pick one to put on a poster, I'd pick you."

"I don't know if that's a compliment or not."

"I think it is."

"Why would you pick me?" She knew she was treading a fine line here between getting his guard down and letting *hers* down.

"Because you look like you could rope and ride as easily and effortlessly as most women could sew a button on a shirt."

"Sew a button on a shirt? Are your views of women that archaic?"

"Beautiful but slightly prickly," he went on, as if she hadn't interrupted.

"I am not." She meant beautiful.

"Believe me prickly is not nearly as deep a character flaw as arrogance."

"That's true."

"You look like you could shoot a bear without blinking—"

"I did so blink. My eyes were shut tight when I pulled the trigger."

He laughed, a good sound, rich and deep, a sound that could chase away a good cowgirl's suspicions. And make her trust someone who had not proven he could be trusted.

"How old were you when you left the ranch?" she asked him.

"Sixteen." The remoteness snapped back into place, but not before she caught a glimpse of regret.

"You miss it." She thought of her time in Edmonton, where not a day had gone by when she didn't miss her brothers' laughter, the warm breath of her horse and being able to walk outside to a space so big you could never fill it, and air so clean and crisp it was like inhaling champagne.

He shrugged, invulnerable. "I suppose. Parts of it."

A note in his voice told her things of him. That he was a long way from the boy who had grown up on a ranch in Wyoming and that he would do anything to find his way back to that kind of simplicity.

Was that how he had found his way here?

No. There was nothing simple about him being here. With a baby who was not his.

"So," she said casually, "what did you do after you left the ranch?"

He came out of the corral, his face completely closed now, hefted the pack boxes, one in each hand, and went back toward the cabin. "This and that," he said. "Saw the world. You know."

But she didn't. And she knew he would not tell her anything further. In this little two-step they were doing to see who could get whose guard down further, she suspected she had just lost round one. She was determined to keep her mouth shut and her eyes open.

Supper was ready in short order. He took over completely, managing the cranky stove like an old hand. Canned stew and biscuits, coffee, strong and hot, and tinned peaches afterward.

"You're used to doing this," she commented.

"Cooking?" he asked.

"Making do. Roughing it."

"This isn't what I would call roughing it," he said, and then looked like he regretted saying it, as if it was a crime to reveal even the tiniest little things about himself to her.

After they'd eaten, they moved out on the porch

with their coffee cups and watched the moon rise over the black silhouette of the mountain. A toad croaked hoarsely, the horses made the odd noise, the rocking chairs squeaked.

"I could stay forever in a place like this," he said, suddenly, quietly, and she had the sensation it was the first truly unguarded thing he had said. "How did you come to be here?"

She ordered her own guard up before she answered. "I like the country," she said. "I like horses."

She left out the part about Edmonton. She left out anything that might make her seem weak, vulnerable or soft. She gave a pretty good account of shooting the renegade grizzly when she was seventeen.

And riding that rank colt of Evan's when no one else could ride him.

Just talk. Nothing about her heart.

Still, she had the awful feeling he was hearing things she was not saying, and she stood up abruptly. "It's cold out. I'm ready to turn in."

"Me, too." He stretched mightily and yawned.

She'd bored him. She should have known.

Storm, she chastised herself, that's the idea. Bore the man near to sleep, and then make your run for it.

When they went back in the cabin, she noticed for the first time that his pack did not have a sleeping bag tied on the frame where one would normally be.

"Where's your bedroll?" she asked.

"I guess I forgot it," he said smoothly.

She had only one sleeping bag with her. She always brought all the bedding down from the cabins at the end of the year to have it laundered, and also to keep the mice out of it over the winter. She had not brought any of it back up yet.

Not that that meant she had to share her bed with him. What a ridiculous thought. They had dozens of options. Dozens. Why had that one leaped so quickly to mind?

Chapter Three

''**O**ne sleeping bag?'' Ben thought a very improper thought about sharing it with her. He hoped his eyebrows weren't waggling away fiendishly like the villain about to tie the poor maiden to the tracks.

"I wasn't expecting company. Maybe you should have brought your own."

Ben had everything a baby could want for a month, including his favorite teddy bear. And not so much as a spare shirt for himself, or a sleeping bag. Bloody stupid to come into this unforgiving country without being prepared. But so far he'd been lucky. Looked after, Noel might have said.

"It doesn't matter," Storm said. "You have the bag. I've got a warm jacket. I'll just curl up on one of the bunks in my jacket."

"The hell you will."

"Do *you* have a warm jacket?" she asked.

"No. It's warm enough in here with that stove going, anyway."

She shrugged but he could tell that while she might give in this time, he had better not make a habit of thinking he was going to run the show.

"My jacket's hanging behind the door if you want to throw it over you."

She picked up the baby and the sleeping bag, thought about it for a minute and handed him the baby.

Before this he had not had much experience with babies sleeping.

He still could not believe how relaxed and floppy their bodies became. Boneless. Like a holding a little warm puddle of skin.

After she had fixed the bunk to her satisfaction, she took Rocky and tucked him in the sleeping bag closest to the wall. She seemed to consider her options, and then hopped in the bag fully dressed.

She turned her back to him, put her arm around Rocky and started to breathe deeply.

Ben glared at her.

She could go to sleep that easily?

He went to the door and looked out. Checking. He listened. Nothing. Night sounds. The faraway cry of a coyote. The hoot of an owl. The wind in the treetops.

The moonlight painted the little clearing silver and black.

There was a sign nailed up on one of the trees. He had glanced at it earlier but now he gave it his full attention. *Heart's Rest.*

He felt it. A deep sense of everything being all right. Safe. In fact, it had been a long, long time since he had felt this safe in the world. He thought of the way he had felt when he touched her horse. Like a man who had been homesick finding his way home.

But he had not been homesick, he reminded himself sternly. He had left that ranch when he was sixteen, and never looked back.

He stepped back into the cabin and closed the door behind him. He glanced over at her. He could just see the top her head. The sleeping bag was rising and falling steadily. Just as a precaution, he looked through her silverware, found a flat knife and inserted it through the doorjamb.

Fighting exhaustion, he went across to the other side of the room and unrolled one of the mattresses tied up on the end of a bunk.

He lay down, fully clothed. His weariness seemed to be turning his bones to lead. Was his stomach feeling slightly queasy, or was that just part of how tired he was? He thought uneasily of some questionable water he had been forced to drink on that wild run out of Crescada. He pushed the thought aside. He could not afford to be sick right now, so he wouldn't be.

Within minutes he was wishing he had a sleeping bag. Or even a jacket.

He got up. That wasn't dizziness, either. Just another symptom of being too long without decent sleep. He went and got her jacket off the door, sat on the edge of the bunk and studied the jacket. Jean, lined with fleece. What part of himself was he supposed to cover with it?

Her jacket smelled tangy, of horses, woods and smoke. And yet it had a deeper aroma clinging to it, too. A clean smell, a fragrance delicate and enticing and pure woman.

He tugged the jacket around him. He had learned to sleep with one eye open—on red alert even as his body rested. He knew he had to sleep. But he felt afraid to let himself go. Afraid of where his dreams would take him, afraid of the deep contentment this isolated cabin made him feel.

That sense of safety he had felt earlier was not a good thing. At all. His eyes closed. Her scent wrapped around him. He slept the deep sleep of a man who had found a resting place for his heart.

Storm waited until his breathing was deep and even, then being careful not to disturb Rocky, who was snoring, she slipped back the covers. Waited. Listened.

Nothing but Rocky's snoring, Ben's deep and even breathing and the crackle of the wood stove.

She sat up, carefully swung her legs out of the bunk and waited again. Strange scents tickled her nostrils. The baby scent.

The man smell.

The cabin was very dark, but she waited and her eyes adjusted to the inkiness. The moon was nearly full tonight, and faint silver chased in the one tiny window. She had a penlight in her jeans pocket no bigger than her finger.

She slipped out of the bunk and across the floor to Ben's pack. She glanced warily at him. He had not struck her as a man who would sleep deeply. But he was asleep, so soundlessly she lifted the pack and crossed the cabin.

She set it down at the door. She was sure she had heard Ben doing something to the door, and she felt along the frame until her fingers hit the knife in the jamb. The door was pried shut. It seemed an unusual precaution to take—up here, so far from anywhere— and it only cemented in her mind that what she was doing now was the only right course of action to take.

She pulled the knife out, glanced back when it squeaked slightly before it came out completely.

His breathing remained deep and even.

That sliver of moonlight illuminated his face slightly. He was a handsome man, and more so at rest, with some of the wariness chased from his features, some of the hardness softened. Was that a sheen of sweat on his forehead? It mustn't be. It wasn't overly hot in the cabin. Just a trick of moonlight.

She opened the door, praying it wouldn't creak. It didn't. She hefted the pack and went out, closing the door softly behind her.

Taking a deep breath she settled herself on the straight-back chair next to the rocker, pulled on her riding boots, which she had left on the porch, undid the flap to the main compartment of the backpack and turned on her little light.

She was not generally a snoop, but something was off here—way off—and she owed it to that baby in there to find out what it was before she left.

She found a full canteen and a map in a waterproof, transparent pouch. Toothbrush. Toothpaste. She was beginning to feel silly, like she was at a house party poking through the host's medicine chest.

She reminded herself it was her house and that she could poke through the medicine chest here if she wanted. Still, the feeling of guilt did not ease, not even when she realized there was no fishing equipment in this pack. Not a single hook so far.

She set the items down carefully, in a line at her

feet, so that she could put them back in in the same order she had taken them out. Then she turned her little penlight back to the task at hand.

Socks. Rough and woolly. Underwear, which made her blush. She would not have pictured him as a boxer man, not that she should be picturing that sort of thing, anyway. No print, thank God, plain navy-blue. She lined up these items beside the others and looked back in. The flashlight glinted off something silver poking out from under a baby's undershirt. She reached in.

Her hand touched something hard and cold. Not wanting it to be what she already knew it was, she pulled it out.

A handgun. Not the kind she'd seen Jake strap on when a rogue bear was known to be about—a big six-shooter Jake wore at the hip, like the guns in old westerns—not that kind at all.

No, this gun was small, sleek and very silver.

She stopped and listened for sounds within the cabin, aware of her pulse beating a wild tempo in her throat.

She knew what she had to do. She had to get on her horse, ride down the trail in the dark and tell the police there was a man at her cabin with a gun and a baby.

But what was she going to do about the baby? She couldn't very well leave Rocky with a dangerous and armed man.

She went no further in the main compartment of the backpack, putting items back in while she thought. And then she noticed another compartment within the main one, almost hidden.

Her fingers felt along the edges of it, until she

found a zipper. She opened it and reached inside. Papers. She flashed her light on them. Passports, two of them. And a foreign document that looked like it might be a driver's license.

The picture was definitely him. Eyes unsmiling, mouth turned down, hair shorter than it was now.

But the name was different than the one he'd given her. Trevor Murdoch. Suspecting already what she would find, she opened the other passport. His picture again. This time his name was Webster Carmichael.

Her mouth was now dry, and her fingers trembling.

She put the papers back in the inside pouch and zipped it closed. She looked around for her shotgun, felt her heart drop even more sickeningly when she saw it was not where she had left it earlier. Quietly, she got up and went down the steps. A chink of rock fell out of one stair and clattered with a noise that seemed deafening to her.

She froze, listened. Nothing. Her heart began to beat again.

She went quietly to where Sam munched away in the moonlight. He lifted his head but did not give his customary nicker.

She'd done it again, really. Thought her suspicions were wild and unreasonable, that she could probably trust this man. This man, who was, apparently, even more a snake than the last one.

She made herself think, focus, while she got her saddle and blankets out of the old tack shed and caught Sam.

Obviously, she couldn't leave Rocky here, a thought that had not once occurred to her during the day when she had outlined her departure in her head.

She was going to have to go back in there and get

him. She didn't want to. She didn't want to risk her escape being foiled. She wanted to swing up on her horse right now and be out of here. Leave the cabin behind her, that man, as if it were a bad dream, as if by riding back down that trail she would be returned to her normal world.

But if she did that, by morning the man and the baby would be gone.

And even though she knew these woods and mountains like the back of her hand, she suspected she would not find him, that no one would find him, if he did not want to be found.

She gave her cinch a final tug and lowered her stirrup leather back down. She slipped the bridle over the halter, and tossed the reins up over the saddle horn. She opened the gate of the pole corral, stopped and contemplated the pack horse. He was going to whinny if she left him here by himself.

She tied Sam, taking extra care with her quick-release knot, and left the gate open. The other horse would probably follow them back down the mountain. The pack horse was the least of her worries at the moment.

Taking a deep breath she forced herself to turn and walk back to the cabin. She hesitated at the wood pile, looking for her ax, and then realized that was gone, too. And realized that it didn't matter, because she doubted she had what it took to hit him with an ax.

Up the stairs, on tiptoe across the creaky old porch. She opened the door just enough to slide through it, paused, feeling blinded by the darkness of the cabin compared to the moonlit clearing.

Nothing had changed.

And everything had changed. The cabin seemed to

be charged with electricity now, fraught with some unknown danger.

She waited for her eyes to adjust to the deeper darkness, looking at his bunk.

It registered in her mind that it was empty just as the hand clamped over her mouth and a strong arm drew her back into him.

"Don't scream. You'll wake Rocky."

She bit down on the flesh of his hand and kicked him hard with the heel of her riding boot. He grunted but his hold on her only tightened.

"Going somewhere?" he asked, his voice a deep growl in her ear.

"Just coming back," she snapped. "You might have noticed no indoor plumbing."

He spun her around, his hands biting strong and hard into her shoulders. The moonlight made his eyes silver, and cold, like ice forming on a creek edge during the first freeze.

"Don't play with me. You can't win."

Just like arm wrestling, and probably just as true this time.

"I don't seem to be the one playing, Mr. *Mc-Kinnon*." Even as she said it, she realized it might have been wiser not to let him know she knew about the other identities, the gun. She wished she hadn't put that gun back in his pack. She wished she would have thought to dismantle it and throw it into the forest.

His hands slipped down from her shoulders and fell to her sides. But his eyes warned her not to try anything. He took his gaze from her for a moment, and she knew he was probing the darkness of the room, looking for his pack.

"Where is it?" he snapped.

"What?" she asked innocently. "My shotgun?"

"Don't test me."

"Test you? You mean like true or false? Is his name Ben McKinnon, true or false? No, he looks much more like a Trevor... no, not Trevor. Webster. Now that's a name that suits him. Webster, just like the dictionary, full of words. Only those words mean something."

The fear seemed to be leaving her, replaced by something white-hot and angry. How dare he come here and try to trick her?

He regarded her coldly and angrily for a moment. Then he looked away, ran a hand through the dark satin of his hair. "You shouldn't have looked in the pack."

"I'm not going to apologize for it. I'm glad I looked. Because you're a liar, Mister whoever-you-are. And maybe a killer. And maybe a kidnapper."

He regarded her thoughtfully, his eyes narrow. "Anything else?" he asked smoothly.

"How about if you tell me?" she snapped back.

"Would you believe anything I said now?"

"No!"

"Well, then I might as well save my breath."

"You got that right."

The baby cried out suddenly, and for a fraction of a second she felt his attention shift from her.

With all her might she plunged into him, pushed him. He staggered backward, and in the split second he was off balance she darted out the cabin door, took the steps in one leap, flew across her little clearing.

She was the fastest runner in Thunder Lake. She

always had been. She won every ribbon at the Canada Day picnic every year. Even against Jake.

She could hear him coming behind her. She knew better than to look back.

My God, he thought, could she ever run. For a moment, he thought he wouldn't catch her, but he knew he couldn't afford to even think it. He was in his socks, and rocks, sticks and other numerous sharp objects kept jabbing him in the feet, but he couldn't afford to think about that, either.

He found some reserve within himself, and pushed. She was nearly at the horse. *A saddled horse.* Damn. With everything he had, he forced an extra burst of speed, and dove at her.

His fingers closed around her ankle and she crashed to the ground. He worried that he had hurt her for only a split second, because she rolled over, writhing like a wildcat. He straddled her, trying to keep the full impact of his weight off her, while still containing her. She wound up and socked him. She packed one hell of a wallop.

He captured one arm and then the other, and pinned them over her head.

He looked down at her. She was panting wildly and glaring at him with blue sparks heating her furious gaze to white-hot.

She wriggled under him, with a mighty effort coiled all her muscles and tried to throw him off. When she failed to move him, she went still as a stone beneath him.

"Are you done?" he asked.

She didn't answer, which he took to be a no. He

wasn't releasing those little but lethal fists until he was pretty sure she wasn't going to hit him with one.

He looked up at the saddled horse just a few feet from them, and cursed himself. She must have been out here for damn near half an hour before he'd woken up and noticed she was missing from the cabin.

"Where were you going?" he asked mildly. *And why had she come back?*

"To get a damn cop!" she spat at him.

He nodded.

"Let go of my arms," she ordered him regally.

"Are you going to hit me again?" His left eye felt like it was starting to swell shut.

She didn't answer, which he took to be a yes. Still, he didn't want to hurt her. Cautiously, he released his hold on her right wrist. She swung immediately, and he caught it just before it clipped him again.

"Storm, I don't want to hurt you."

"That's what everybody with a gun in their backpack says!"

"Okay, you don't have a single reason to trust me. I know that. But listen to me. Look in my eyes and listen to me, and listen to what your heart tells you."

Where the hell was that in the manual? he wondered briefly. Listen to what your heart tells you?

"My name really is Ben McKinnon. And I'm not going to hurt you. Or Rocky. How could I hurt Rocky?"

She was looking at him so intensely he thought he might drown in the soft blue pools of her eyes. He realized he felt warm beyond what his little chase merited. Was she making him feel all hot and bothered? He actually felt feverish.

He felt something relax in her underneath him. He let go of her hands. She didn't swing.

"Could you get off of me?"

He did, carefully, making sure he had a hold of her shoulder before he took his weight completely off her. He helped her sit up. She was covered in dirt and twigs, and he brushed awkwardly at the worst of it on her back.

"Don't," she said, swatting at him.

He held out his hand to her and helped her to her feet. He didn't let go of her hand when she stood up. That saddled horse was just a little too close.

"I need to know the truth," she said, her voice small but stubborn, too.

He looked at her, *wanted* to tell her. Very professional. He knew he needed to think before he told her anything. And right now he wasn't thinking straight at all. He still felt light-headed, feverish. Because of the way her hand felt in his? More likely from the way she had socked him moments ago.

Without releasing her hand, he moved over to the horse. With his right hand, he flipped the stirrup up and loosened the latigo.

"You can let go of me."

If she went into these woods at night, it would take him a good long time to find her, though there was not a doubt in his mind that he would.

But what if the baby needed something while he was out pushing through the bush looking for her? Instead of letting her go, he tightened his hold on her.

She tried to twist out of his grasp.

He pulled the saddle off, still with just his right hand, ignoring her mutinous look. He dumped it on the ground. Even with everything on his mind, he liked the saddle, a good one, quality leather, the scent filling his nostrils. He knew full well this was no way to treat a good saddle.

Or a good woman.

Without releasing her, he took off the bridle, sliding it out gently so as not to bang it on old Sam's teeth. Funny, how something like that, how to take out a bridle, stayed with you for a lifetime, was there even when you thought you'd moved way beyond it. He shooed the horse back into the corral. The other one followed happily and he shut the gate.

"You can let me go now," she said again.

"All right."

She rubbed her hand as if he'd hurt her, and he felt a stab of regret and realized he wanted her to like him. A weakness. He couldn't care about what she thought about him and do his job, too.

He braced himself for her to dart one way or the other, but she didn't.

Instead she stood there looking at him with her eyes full of accusation and anger, her chest rising and falling rapidly under the faded plaid of her shirt.

He forced his voice to be flat, cold and uncaring. "Let's go. I need to get some sleep."

He waited for her to turn and go, then fell into step right behind her. Her nose was tilted up toward the stars.

She went up the cabin steps, pulled off her boots, marched in the door ahead of him. Without so much as a backward glance, she went and pulled back the sleeping bag and crawled in beside the baby, who after his one ill-timed wail seemed to have settled right back to sleep.

Now what? Sit in a chair and watch her all night?

He couldn't. Because she would wake up refreshed and he would be dead tired. He was going to need his wits about him. Besides, he felt as if he physically couldn't stay awake much longer. That leaden feeling had returned to his limbs.

If he told her the truth, would she believe it? He doubted it. It sounded wild and improbable, a plot for a spy movie.

He went and pulled the narrow mattress off the bed he'd been sleeping on. And then another one off the top bunk. He put them together on the floor.

"Storm." He snapped it out, an order.

She turned and looked at him warily, defiantly.

"Bring Rocky over here."

"Why?"

"Because I said so."

"Oh, and you're the one with the gun."

"That's right."

She picked up Rocky, and he could not miss the worry in her expression as she tucked the little sleeping baby close to her.

He knew suddenly that was why she had come back. She could have been on that horse and gone, but she had worried about Rocky.

A baby that was not hers. That she barely knew.

It made him feel a stab of tenderness for her. But she might perceive that as weakness and so he did not let it show. Instead he pointed at the mattress and used that drill sergeant tone that brooked no argument.

"Lie down."

"No."

"Storm, I'm tired and I'm cranky, and I'm two

seconds from trussing you up like a chicken. Lie down.''

She tossed her head mutinously, settled the baby on the mattress, spared him a look that would have killed a lesser man, and lay down beside the baby.

Ben retrieved the sleeping bag from the bunk. He undid the zipper, turning it into a big comforter, rather than a bag, and tossed it over her and Rocky.

He could wait until she went to sleep and then crawl in beside them.

Of course, he might wake up to another black eye.

Better just to face the music now.

He sat down on the edge of the mattress, his back to her, and pulled off his socks, grimy from running around outside in them. He sensed her stillness. She had stopped breathing, waiting to see what he would do.

He checked his feet for cuts, found none, and pulled off his shirt. It was too hot in here.

He heard her soft intake of breath.

He pulled back a corner of the sleeping bag and slid in beside her.

She gasped softly. ''What do you think you're doing?''

''I'm going to sleep,'' he said, reaching under the sleeping bag until he found her hand. He locked his hand around her wrist.

''Oh!'' she sputtered. ''Let go of me!''

He complied, flipped over on his side, and threw his whole arm over her soft midriff. ''Better?'' he growled.

He peered at her from under the cover of his lashes. She was staring angrily at the ceiling. Her body was coiled with tension.

His priority was only to find a solution. She wanted to run. He couldn't let her. Short of tying her up, this was the best he could do.

But he hadn't expected to feel this.

To feel her vulnerability and her fear.

To feel the softness of her curves so close to him.

To feel her scent teasing his nostrils.

Could life really get much more unfair than this?

After a while he felt her relax slightly and dared to look. Her lashes were long and sooty like chimney-sweeping brushes. Her lips were faintly parted. She hated him.

How could a man be this close to a beautiful woman and not have a thing happen?

He shot a baleful glance heavenward. Okay. Okay. It could get more unfair after all.

Chapter Four

Storm awoke to darkness, listening.

A bear? She had heard a growl, or a moan.

It all came back to her in a flash. The man appearing at her cabin, the baby, the gun in his knapsack, the fact she was now a prisoner.

She would be tempted to dismiss it all as an unpleasant dream, except for the reality of the baby nestled into her. His tuft of hair tickled her chin. She touched his chest and was reassured by the rise and fall of it.

Her eyes were adjusting to the inky darkness now. It must have clouded over since her escape attempt, she realized, as moonlight no longer washed the small room.

Her escape attempt. She felt fresh anger rising in her, until she realized that his arm no longer held her captive under its weight, that no strong fingers bit into her wrist.

She turned slowly, cautiously, over.

The place where he had slept was empty.

Her heart began to race. Now was the time to go. "He who hesitates is lost," and she had no intention of being lost.

She got to her feet. Her eyes adjusted to the murkiness. He was not in the cabin. At the outhouse, then. She had a five- or ten-second window of time. Maybe she wouldn't bother with the saddle this time, just go bareback down the mountain as fast as she could.

But it was really dark now, and the going would be treacherous. With the baby she had to think differently than she would think if she were going on her own.

That sound again. She froze, listening.

It was like a moan, a deep and pained growl, but not a sound like she had ever heard a bear make.

She noticed the cabin door was slightly ajar, went over to it on silent feet and peered out the crack. He was sitting on the porch, his head cradled in his hands. He was holding *her* boots hostage right beside him! The fink.

He made that sound again, and she felt a strange shiver go up and down her spine. Now what? Take the baby and try to run by him in her sock feet? Go back to bed? *What?*

She listened for that still, small voice inside her that had guided her so unerringly through the days of her life, that had let her down only once.

Go outside.

She frowned, looking for something a little more dramatic. Grab the kitchen knife. Light the cabin on fire and, while he is putting it out, slip away down the mountain. Squeeze out the window.

She glanced at the window. Even if she could

squeeze through it without getting stuck, what was she supposed to do with the baby? Drop him through first?

Go outside.

Sighing, telling the voice it was wrong, she opened the door and stepped out.

His head flew up.

It was slightly lighter out here, and she stared at him. Despite the chill in the night air, his face was bathed in perspiration. His shirt was stuck to his body in dark patches.

He was sick. Really sick. His eyes, so clear, steady and stern just hours before looked glazed and unfocused.

She was willing to bet she could waltz right by him with the baby and he wouldn't have the strength or presence of mind to stop her.

He got to his feet, but she could see he was wobbly. He took a step toward her that was more like a lurch, and then, like a big tree that had been felled, he swayed and toppled.

Right at her feet.

She nudged him with her sock, and he groaned but did not move.

Well, that made life easy. Get the baby and go.

But what if she came back to a dead man on her porch? What if the wound that she had cleaned had become infected? Sighing, she went back into the cabin, picked up her first-aid kit and lit the lantern. She brought it back out. He did not stir in the pool of light.

The lantern made his face have a faintly greenish tinge.

"McKinnon?" She crouched down beside him.

"Ben?" He stirred slightly. She tried out his other names but got no response to them. Maybe his name really *was* Ben McKinnon.

She tugged up the shirt. It was soaked with sweat. The heat coming off his skin was fearsome. She didn't even want to guess what his temperature might be.

She took the scissors out of her kit and cut away the careful bandages she had wrapped him up in earlier. She was relieved to see the wound looked clean. It had bled some more, but there was no festering or redness around it. The bandages smelled clean. She rewrapped it as best she could, taping down the edges.

His eyes flicked open as she lay her hand across his forehead, which was burning hot. He stared at her, then reached out and grabbed her ankle.

"You're not going anywhere," he informed her thickly. "Don't even think it."

She unlocked his fingers. He had no fight in him. She wasn't about to have a battle of wits with an unarmed man.

"I'm going to take off your shirt," she told him, amazed at the gentleness in her tone. He'd been her *captor,* for Pete's sake! "You're going to have to help. I'm going to sponge you off with some cool water, and then get some aspirin into you. Then I'm leaving."

He groaned. "Water."

"I'll get you some, in just a minute. That's a good idea. Liquids, lots of—"

"Water I drank," he muttered.

"You drank water that wasn't safe? Is that what you're telling me?"

He took her sleeve. "Crescada," he said.

Crescada. It seemed to her that was some small country halfway around the world that she had never even heard of until a month or so ago. Some kind of unrest, because they were planning a free election for the first time in their history, had earned them fifteen seconds on the news every now and then.

"You drank water in Crescada?" she probed.

He closed his eyes. His breathing was coming in shallow pants.

"Ben." She got a flicker of recognition this time. She had to ask one more thing before he slipped away from her. "Did the baby drink any of that water? Did you give Rocky any of that water?"

He opened his eyes and looked at her with furious indignation. "Bottled water for him." His gaze clouded again. His voice died away.

She pondered that for a moment.

He had managed to find clean water for the baby. He had put the welfare of the baby ahead of his own.

For that, and only for that, she would make sure she got his fever down before she tied him up. What was his expression? Oh yes, she'd truss him up like a chicken. If his temperature had not been quite so worrisome, it might have been one of life's more satisfying moments.

With a strange calm, she went and dampened several facecloths and crushed aspirin into juice.

She went back out onto the porch with a basin of water and a towel slung over her shoulder.

His eyes were open again. He was staring at the sky.

"Ben?" she said, getting on her knees beside him, "I'm going to sponge you off—"

He grabbed her arm with frightening strength and looked hard at her. "Where's Noel?" he demanded.

She extricated her arm and pulled back his shirt, wrestling one of his arms from a sleeve, and then the other. She patted his chest with a damp dishcloth, not at all indifferent to the magnificence of it, even though he had behaved terribly toward her. She felt that should make a difference, and a large one, in the way she reacted to him, but it didn't seem to. At all.

Closer to animals than we are prepared to admit, she thought, aware of a deep and burning hunger in her as she touched his chest so intimately.

"Tell me about Noel," she suggested. In his weakened state he was more likely to reveal things about himself that she wanted to know. As long as in her weakened state she could digest them.

"Such a good man," he croaked. "A better man than me. Believed in love. Life. Believed people were good." He snorted in derision at that. "Believed we had a purpose here." He swore, his pain evident, and then his eyes went wild. "Where's Noel?"

"Crescada?" she guessed, running the washcloth over the firm muscles of his chest, watching the water bead in the dark hair that curled on his chest.

His eyes darkened, and he stared at her. "Noel's dead, isn't he?"

"I don't know, Ben. I sure hope not."

She had mixed the aspirin in with apple juice. He closed his lips firmly and eyed her warily.

"Come on," she said. "Open up."

He glared at her.

"Please?"

Nothing.

It was ridiculous, and yet she knew exactly what to do. "Chugga-chugga choo-choo," she sang softly.

A light came on in his eyes that she had not seen before. He opened his mouth and swallowed the aspirin and juice with a sigh. She finished bathing him, a sweet torture. He was so hot that the water seemed to evaporate as soon as it touched him. She felt she should get him inside, out of the cool night air, but she had no way of moving him without his cooperation, and it didn't look as if he planned to cooperate.

He was not a cooperating kind of guy, even in health. He closed his eyes, and after a while his breathing became deep and steady.

She decided she would wait half an hour to make sure his temperature had gone down before she took the baby and left. Meanwhile, she would find her shotgun and get rid of his pistol.

Then again, if Noel, whoever that was, was dead, how had he died? And under what circumstances? Maybe she had better not get rid of the pistol too prematurely.

She went over to his backpack and rummaged through it at leisure, looking more carefully at the IDs. He looked, she decided, very formidable in these pictures, stern and unyielding. And yet the carefully folded little baby clothes, the fact there was a teddy bear in here—the ear nearly worn off from being so thoroughly chewed—told her something else about him.

Her hand rested on the gun, and she reluctantly pulled it out. She thought it was a particularly evil-looking device. Handguns had only one purpose. They were useless for hunting because their range was so short. No, all a pistol was good for was causing harm to another human being. It was hard to reconcile that with the teddy bear. Holding it gingerly between her index finger and her thumb, she went over to a place in the porch floor where a board was loose, pulled it up and set the pistol down in the darkness.

She checked Ben, who seemed quite a bit cooler, and then went and searched for her shotgun.

She finally found it as dawn was coming up, piercing the sky with its beautiful pink fingers.

Back on the porch, Ben was now shivering. Storm went into the cabin, checked on the baby in the sleeping bag and found herself a few sturdy lengths of rope.

But when she came back out, Ben was at the porch railing, heaving over the side.

He turned to her, finally, and gave her a look that held no recognition.

"Noel's dead," he said flatly.

She didn't know what to say. She tucked the rope into her back pocket. "I'm sorry," she said.

"Where's the baby? Where's Rocky?" There was a trace of panic in his voice, and for some reason it made her ashamed of the rope in her back pocket.

"He's sleeping. Ben, he's fine. The baby is fine."

He looked away, his gaze distant. "His dad said that sometimes if you wanted something badly enough, you could pay for it with your life."

"Well, how could you have it if you were dead?"

"He wanted it for the baby."

"What?"

His voice was very weak. He staggered over to her chair and collapsed in it. "He wanted a different life for his baby."

She went to him and touched his forehead. The heat was coming back. She went back into the cabin and mixed some more fruit juice and aspirin. Her window of opportunity was going to close if she did not slip through it now.

She suspected she was going to have to forget tying him up, take her chances.

She went and spooned the aspirin into him. He barely moved.

The baby woke up, and she fed and changed him. She tucked him under her arm, grabbed her shotgun and went out the door.

She glanced at Ben.

He looked pretty rough.

She took the baby down the path to her horse corral and set him on the grass beside the corral. Her nerves were strung tight as piano wire, and the horses recognized it. Even old Sam, who never spooked from anything, was looking around warily, sensing her edginess and reacting to it. Even when she tried to reassure him, her voice came out shaky. Every knot seemed too hard to do up. She dropped the bridle. Sam didn't want to take the bit.

Finally, she was ready. She went and picked up the baby, propped him into the saddle, then leaped up behind him.

Nothing could stop her now. Nothing.

She rode up to the cabin, just to check Ben one more time.

He was at the railing again, looking at her with eyes that were confused and full of pain.

"Storm," he said, "don't go, please."

She was amazed that he recognized her and wondered if that meant he was coming out of his daze enough to be dangerous.

"I have to," she said.

"They might come after him, you know."

"What? Who might come after who?"

"The men who killed Noel, Rocky's dad. They might come after Rocky."

She stared at him. "Are you telling me there are people trying to kill this baby?"

"It's a possibility."

"You're joking."

"No, ma'am, I'm not."

Something about the way he said that sent a shiver up and down her spine. She stared at him, trying to think.

"I'll tell you everything. And then if you decide to go, I won't stop you. I promise."

Storm glared at him. She knew what a man's promise was worth. Precisely nothing. Well, not all men. Her brothers were rare examples of trustworthiness in the male species.

"If you're such a man of honor," she said, backing the horse away from the porch, "why didn't you just tell the whole story straight out?"

He was holding that railing so tightly, to keep himself from falling over, that she almost felt sorry for him. Almost.

"I couldn't."

"But you can now."

"You've got the whip hand now," he admitted.

"Why couldn't you tell me before?"

"I didn't think you needed to know."

"You invade my cabin, you take me prisoner, you—"

"Look, Storm, I admit it. I lied to you. I'm not here on vacation. But there are reasons I lied. Now you either choose to stay or ride away, but make your choice now, because I'm not going to stand here while you call me every name in the book."

"I wasn't going to call you *every* name in the book."

"Mostly," he said thickly, "because I can't stand." And with that he somersaulted over the railing, landed face first in her little flower bed, stirred and groaned. She'd seen enough men tossed off broncs and bulls to know it would take a little more than that to seriously hurt him.

Still, she stared at him, and then looked at where the trail left the clearing, wound down the mountain. Her head told her to make for the trail.

Her heart told her, *stay*.

The baby had a fistful of the horse's mane and was bending over trying to cram it into his mouth.

His hair was standing straight up in a funny little point, and she smoothed it down, touched the roundness of his cheeks.

Someone trying to kill Rocky? What kind of world was this, anyway?

And then she knew why Ben had come here. Because whatever kind of world it was, this little clearing seemed like it was separate from that. A place of mountain and sky, of towering hemlock and thick pine. A place of delicate flowers and starlit nights. A place where the air was so clean and crisp it was like inhaling champagne.

It was a place that honored things larger than men, their pettiness, the guns they carried in their backpacks.

It was, in all the world, a safe place.

And if someone was trying to kill Rocky, he needed this safe and sacred haven. And he needed Ben. She wouldn't know how to protect him if she had to. But Ben would. It didn't seem likely that she would have to, not in Thunder Lake. But she had no way of knowing who was looking for the baby, how far-reaching their influence might be, how far they might have followed Ben.

Ben had not trusted the authorities with the baby. Why was that? What if she put her trust in the authorities and they failed?

Sighing, she placed the baby's hands on the saddle horn, swung her leg over his head and dismounted. She tugged him down beside her. Still, she decided she would leave Sam tacked and ready to go. She tied him to a nearby tree.

She stepped over the inert body in the flower bed and put the baby on her jacket on the porch. Then she went out to try to get Ben out of the dirt. She finally managed to get his arm slung around her shoulder and, with him semi-cooperative, made it into the cabin. She put him in a lower bunk and tossed the sleeping bag over him. All day he talked in incoherent bits and pieces. She sponged him off, forced liquids into him and listened.

That night she brought the rocking chair in and she and the baby slept under her jacket.

She was giving the baby some of those horrible slimy peas for his breakfast when Ben staggered to the table and sat down.

She eyed him critically. "You look as if you've been into the moonshine."

"And feel like it," he said.

"Breakfast?"

"I'm not quite ready to push my luck."

"You've heard of my cooking, then."

He managed a weak smile. "Nothing personal. Storm, did I thank you yet for not leaving?"

"Let's see. You thanked me for knitting you the sweater with the bear on it. Your favorite Christmas gift."

"Good God, that was my grandmother! I was five or six. If you didn't know about the bear, I wouldn't believe it."

"Oh, there's more. You thanked me for letting you put the weak colt, Jasper, behind the stove in the kitchen."

"That was my mom, and I was nine."

"And you thanked me for your first kiss."

A funny little stain of brick-red actually moved up his neck, but she doubted it was a result of the fever coming back.

"Betty-Lou Montgomery. Grade Seven. You don't look anything like Betty-Lou."

"Or your mother or grandmother, I hope!"

"Well, maybe a little bit like Granny. Right around the eyes."

Though his face remained impassive, she saw he was kidding. "Careful, mister, or I'll wrestle you to the ground and soundly trounce you. And I don't think it would take much."

"No," he agreed. He reached over and tickled the baby's ear. Rocky grinned a little green grin at him, and Ben grinned back.

"And by the way, no you did not thank me for not leaving, and with good reason. I haven't not left yet. I'm just waiting to hear what you have to say." But somehow, listening to his fevered rambling, her mind was closer to being made up than she was going to let on. She had a feeling of knowing him.

"I've been really out of it. Did I say anything else interesting?"

"Like state secrets?"

"Yeah, something like that."

"I wished, but no, you are about as much a mystery as the moment you appeared. You didn't get much beyond age sixteen. Except for Noel."

Pain flashed through his eyes, and for a moment he shut them. He took a deep breath and reopened them. "What did I say about Noel?"

"That he was Rocky's dad. That he was dead. And that it was your fault."

"Ah."

"I need to hear it, Ben. All of it. You promised, and I'm ready."

"All right. My name really is Ben."

"I know that. You didn't answer to either of the other two."

He looked at her thoughtfully. "I work for an agency of the American government called the Federal Intelligence Agency."

"Like the CIA?"

"A relative."

"Can you prove it?"

He undid a snap on a deep pocket on his pant leg and slid out a thin folder. It was a very official looking ID. Another picture of him looking grim and stern.

She looked at it very carefully, then passed it back to him.

"A few months ago I was asked to go to Crescada,

to help set up the first democratic elections there. My job, specifically, was to guard the life of the only man who had the guts to run against the candidate put forward by the family who has run that country since the beginning of time. It's not the kind of assignment I usually take, but for some reason I did."

"Noel East," she guessed.

His features clouded. "He'd just lost his wife. She died having Rocky. I sometimes wondered if he ran because he had nothing left to live for once she was gone."

"Except the baby!"

"He had this funny notion about the baby."

"I think you told me that part."

"Did I?"

"Was it that he could have his wish for his child if he gave up his life for it?"

"Yeah."

"And his wish for Rocky was for a better life for him?"

"Noel wanted things for his son that we take so much for granted. Freedom. Prosperity. Honestly, Storm, you don't even know what we have on this continent until you go other places."

"Underneath that deeply cynical front, are you hiding the heart of a man who wants to make the world a better place?" she asked.

"I didn't think I was that cynical."

"Jaded might be better."

"I guess I didn't know I had become that either."

"Tell me what happened next."

"It was my night off. Noel's party posted guard. The guard shot him."

"Someone who was supposed to protect him?"

"Yes."

"Oh, Ben!"

"Have you heard enough? There's a big, bad world beyond this one, Storm."

"I happen to know that," she said sharply. "What does all this have to do with the baby?"

He sighed. "The ruling party might want to make it very plain they don't want anyone to step up and take Noel's place."

"By killing his baby?"

"Wouldn't that make you hesitate to choose politics as a career in Crescada? Putting your whole family on the line?"

"I don't believe it."

"They sure as hell were taking shots at me when I was trying to get him out of there."

"It is a gunshot."

"I was lucky. A graze."

"How long will they look for the baby?"

"The whole country was on the verge of civil war when I got out. I don't know. I have feelers out. Within a week, I'll have a plan in place that will keep Rocky safe if he's not now."

"And you don't believe he is."

"No."

"How did you get out?"

"That's a whole different story. I crossed into a neighboring country through the jungle, used some contacts to have papers manufactured for him and chose between a flight going to Iceland or one coming to Canada. I'd been to Canada before."

"When you were a boy. So you really were here?"

"Yes."

"So if I agree to stay here, it would be for a week?"

"I have a radio stashed in the bush. I'll be checking in a week to see what my status is. I'll be moving on."

"Did anyone follow you?"

"No. But obviously there were other passengers on that plane. You never know."

"Why didn't you just go to the Canadian authorities as soon as you landed?"

"Noel was killed by a man I trusted. I didn't want to trust anyone else, not for a while. I made Noel a promise."

"And that was?"

"That I would take care of his boy. That I would see Rocky had a better life than he did, a different one."

She searched his face. He looked back at her steadily.

"Now could I ask you a few questions?" he asked.

"That wasn't part of the deal."

"Is your real name Storm?"

She smiled. "No, it's Shauna. But I was born in the shadow of this mountain and I have a bit of a temper. My brothers started calling me that, and never quit."

"A bit of a temper?" he said. "Look at this." He pointed to the bruise up his cheek where her fist had caught him.

"Okay, a bit more than a bit of a temper. I was raised by my brothers," she found herself telling him. "My parents died in a fire."

"I'm sorry."

"It's okay. I was too young to remember it. My brothers are pretty great guys. You'd like them."

Oddly enough, given the circumstances, she was almost sure her brothers would like Ben, too.

"Can I ask you one more question?"

She shrugged. "Sure, I guess."

"Who hurt you?"

She stiffened as if he'd slapped her. His first question had been so innocent; nothing had prepared her for this one.

"You're the one with the bruises," she said. "I'm not hurt."

He didn't back down. "A man?"

She looked away, stunned that he could see it.

"What did he do?" he asked softly.

Without knowing why, she told him. "Married."

"He was married?"

She nodded, still not looking at him.

His fingers touched her chin, guided her eyes back to his. "Did you know he was married?"

"Of course not! He didn't tell me."

"That snake," Ben said with soft and killing contempt.

"What do you care?"

"I want you to know not all men are like that."

"Thank you. I think I figured that out."

"Is that why you're hiding back here in the hills?"

"I am not hiding!"

"There are lots of ways to hide."

"Is that right? And is Crescada one of them?"

He smiled slightly. "I suppose it might be."

"Why are you doing this?"

"Because a time might come when you have to trust me, and I need you to know I'm not like him."

"Oh, sure. The guy with a selection of names."

"Your friend who was married only had one name, am I right?"

"Your point?"

"Sometimes your heart can tell you more than your head."

"I'll stay for a week. The baby needs me. Maybe you do, too. But don't ask me to trust you."

"What if your life depended on it? Would you trust me then?"

She looked into his eyes. The quiet strength in them could not be denied. "I think I could trust you then."

"In that case, can I have my gun back?"

Chapter Five

"You want your gun back?"

Ben could see it had been a mistake to ask. Every bit of territory he had just won was lost again, the mistrust brilliant in her eyes.

"I think it would be a good idea if I had it," he said, and then addressed her fear. "What do you think I'm going to do with it?"

"Why don't you tell me?"

"I'm going to use it if the bad guys show up. I think you know you have nothing to fear from me. You practically know my whole life history—the bear sweater, Jasper, Betty-Lou."

"Your whole life history ended at age sixteen?" she said skeptically.

That was more true than she knew. His parents had split up when he was sixteen. It had been the beginning of shutting down his feelings. He'd been attracted to his line of work because it actually *required* him to turn off his emotional side, to suppress anything in him that needed anything as nebulous as tenderness or nurturing.

"The baby needs a bath," she said, the discussion about the gun apparently over, for now. "Do you know how to bath a baby?"

"Not a baby, but I did have a puppy once."

"I know, his name was Caboo."

"Do I have any secrets left?"

"You tell me."

He leaned over and wiped the green dribbles off Rocky's chin with his sleeve. He did have a secret left. At least he hoped he did. This baby made him *feel* things. A funny ache, a strange yearning. For a path not chosen. For a life not quite so devoid of warmth.

The embarrassing truth was that even her horse made him feel things: a strange longing for a lifestyle he thought he had left behind him. Way behind him. But his fevered dreams had been full of memories of that young colt behind the stove, of long and simple days spent in the saddle.

The frightening truth was that Storm Taylor made him feel things he didn't even want to think about.

"I think you know all my secrets," he lied, one of those necessary lies.

"What kind of name is Caboo for a dog?" she asked, and reached over with a washcloth to get the dribbles he had missed.

"It's a darn good name for a dog. He was the last one of the litter, kind of like the caboose."

"And what happened to him? You called for him over and over."

He was silent. The dog had been one of the things he had left behind when he left the ranch. He knew he had never dealt with any of that pain but he hadn't known that it was waiting deep in his psyche for a vulnerable moment.

Now he wondered how much the loss of his dad, his dog and his boyhood ranch home had to do with him wandering the face of the earth, cynically refusing what other men had. Homes. Families. He decided he was in a weakened state to allow himself such thoughts.

He leaped up from the table. "Bathing Rocky won't be that different from bathing the pup," he told her, taking charge. "We'll need warm water and soap. I have special soap for him."

He went to his pack and rummaged around, laying out a little clean undershirt and more pajamas with feet in them. He found the bar of Especially-for-Baby soap that he had bought—along with the formula and the baby food—at one of his few stops on his way here.

"See," he said, handing her the soap, "this soap is formulated for baby's skin."

"You read the label on a bar of soap? Did you pay this for it?" She was staring at the price tag incredulously.

He glared at her.

"They saw you coming."

"His skin is very delicate!" He knew what she'd done immediately. Walked him into a trap. Made him admit how much he cared about that squirming little bundle of life. He tried to hide the tiny bottle of Especially-for-Baby shampoo he'd bought, but she came and took it right out of his hand.

But at least she was smiling now. Maybe she'd

even give him back the gun. He decided to wait until after the bath to ask her.

A bath under these conditions was a bigger undertaking than he could have imagined. She kept putting more containers of water on the stove, and stoking it up until she had the stove glowing red-hot—and the cabin warmer than a Finnish sauna.

"He's not that big!" Ben finally protested, as she pumped water into yet another bucket.

"But you are."

"Pardon?"

"We're giving him a bath, and then you're having one."

He scowled at her. Since when was she giving the orders? She turned and smiled at him.

Okay, so he needed a bath.

Soon they had a little metal tub filled halfway with lukewarm water. She handed him Rocky.

"You're the expert on bathing puppies," she reminded him, folding her arms across her chest and watching.

He took off Rocky's little sleeper and his diaper, then set him gently in the basin.

Rocky smiled happily and began to splash with wild enthusiasm.

"You've got to hang on to him tight," he told her. "He'll get away from you in a second if you don't."

"And what would he do, swim away?"

He glared at her. She obviously had no idea what a serious undertaking this was. She had a hand in the water now and was splashing water on the baby, who was crowing with delight and splashing her back.

Soon, they were all pretty wet, that baby getting

slipperier and slipperier as Ben added the Especially-for-Baby soap to the equation.

"Quit splashing," Ben ordered her, over the happy shouts of the baby. "Can't you see, I'm trying to get a job done?"

She splashed him! Right in the eye.

He stared at her, his hands full of slippery baby. He freed a hand. She stepped back, but not quickly enough.

He let fly and his hand hit the water, soaking the front of her shirt.

She grinned and went to the stove. She tested the water.

"Not too hot," she called, picking up a whole bucket.

"Hey! I've got a baby here."

She was advancing on him.

"You'll be sorry," he told her.

She did not look the least threatened.

"You'll have to clean the floor!" he told her. When she didn't get it, he made it clear. "Women worry about their floors, damn you!"

"This old floor could probably use a bit of water."

Whoosh. She let fly, and the water went over him like a wave, drenching him. He did his best to protect the baby, who let him know he didn't need protection by gurgling with delight and flailing his arms.

"I'm going to get you," he promised her.

She laughed.

He wished she wouldn't do that. She was a woman made for a man to share laughter with. It made him feel a killing rage at the man who had hurt her.

Married. How could a man do that to a woman like her? How? He thought he'd dealt with some of the world's worst slimeballs but obviously he was mistaken.

She was getting the other bucket off the stove!

"Hey," he said, taking the slippery baby out of the water and tucking him in close to him. "Enough is enough!"

She was still coming.

He made a dash for the door but caught the water right in the middle of his back. "Okay," he said, "this is war."

The baby chortled. So did she.

He carefully wrapped the baby in a towel. He did it slowly, taking his time, making her anticipate his next move. He set Rocky on their makeshift mattress on the floor which, miraculously, was not wet yet. He turned back, fully expecting to see her cowering in the corner, her nerves taut from thinking over what his revenge might be.

Instead, she had commandeered the bathwater and was grinning wickedly! That had been his plan!

He came right at her. No more running away. The enemy had obviously interpreted that as a sign of weakness. They had a brief struggle over the bathwater, which he won. He took the tub and poured it right over her head.

She was howling with laughter, the water cascading down around her. She pushed in close to him so that the water would hit him, too.

She wrapped her arms right around him, so he had no choice. If he continued, he was going to soak himself, too. He was no more worried about a soaking than she had been worried about her floors.

He continued. A sane man would have stopped.

He was not sure when, in his entire life, he had had

a moment so utterly delicious as this one. Her wet body pressed into his, shaking with laughter.

The tub emptied. She started to break away from him, but he wrapped his arms around her and picked her up.

She was beautiful, her hair wet and scattered around her face, beads of water dripping off her nose and chin, laughter in her eyes.

"What are you doing?" she demanded.

"I swore I saw a horse trough out there."

"You wouldn't!"

"Why not?" He strode toward the door.

"It's cold!"

"All's fair in war." He deliberately left out the love part.

"Ben!" She was squirming in his arms now, trying to get free.

"Maybe we could make a deal," he said, halfway to the horse corral.

"What?" she said, still trying to break free. She was one strong woman. At least she wasn't slugging him. She thought he was going to ask about the gun again, because her eyes went all wary. She'd been right, but he changed tack now, deciding to surprise her.

"You change diapers the rest of today."

"That's a hard bargain."

"Take it or leave it."

They were at the corral now. The horses were chewing complacently, watching with interest. He dipped her down. Her hair trailed in the water. She clutched at him.

"Take it or leave it," he said with menace.

"I will not sell my soul!" she cried. Taking him

totally off guard she wrapped her arms and legs around him and threw her weight backward.

It was because he tried, at the last moment, to do the gentlemanly thing and hold her out of the water that he went into the trough with her.

The water was freezing. It was an absolute shock. Not to mention her flailing around with his weight on top of her. He leaped to his feet and pulled her up. They stood in the trough staring at each other, dripping water.

Her clothes were absolutely molded to her.

"You are a hellcat," he told her.

"My brothers don't call me Storm because of my meek nature," she admitted.

She shook her great mane of dark hair and the water flew everywhere. Sam came over and slowly rolled his head to get a good long look at her, then at him.

Ben started to laugh. She was shivering now, paying for her fierce pride and spirit. He pulled her into his arms, which was something of a mistake because her body was soft and pliable and seemed to fit into the curve of his in just the right way.

She was laughing now, too, her head buried in his shoulder.

He realized they had needed this. The last two nights had been too tense for her. With him appearing out of nowhere, taking her captive, getting sick, her taking him captive.

To play like this, to be carefree after a lifetime lived in deadly seriousness, seemed to be just what he needed, and particularly after all the horror of the last days. All the strain. Just to feel alive again. To know it was possible to laugh.

Since neither of them was a prisoner anymore it

was time to start phase two: two wounded people had to learn to trust again.

Good luck.

He wondered if now might be a good time to ask for the gun. He decided maybe not right now, when things were so good.

He set her down. He wished he would have bargained for his gun, instead of a mere day of diaper changing, not that he'd gotten that, either. He noticed she was in her socks and that they were as soaked as the rest of her. With a sigh, he picked her up and sloshed across the yard.

"Put me down!" she said.

"And ruin a perfectly good pair of socks!"

"I don't care about the stupid socks. Put me down!"

"Nope."

"You are a really stubborn man."

"Oh, I'm the stubborn one. All you had to do was agree to change diapers!"

"I had a mule just like you once."

"And what was his name?"

"I'm pretty sure it was Ben."

"It was not."

"Okay, maybe it was Moe."

"How is that similar to Ben?"

"They both have three letters in them."

"See? Just plain stubborn. Moe is a terrible handle for a mule. And you thought Caboo was a bad name." He gave his head a sorrowful shake, thoroughly enjoying this light banter.

He could not remember feeling so carefree, so light. Not for many, many years. He tried to think when, and remembered coming to this cabin once before. With his father, on a hunting trip.

Just the two of them, free at last of the weight of his mother's unhappiness. They had not hunted successfully, but laughed together, built fires, played cards, hiked in these mountains.

He looked around the clearing and could not help but wonder if this space did hold something sacred within it.

"Now you're an expert on naming mules? Is there anything you are not an expert on?" she demanded.

Well, yes there was. He was no expert on matters of the heart. But he wasn't about to tell her that. Hell, he probably already had.

He set her down inside the cabin door. She went over to the baby and lifted him up above her head. It made her wet shirt mold to her in the most unfortunate way.

Together they finished getting the baby dressed and mopped up the cabin. They put more water on the stove to heat for the next bath.

Then she ducked behind the curtain and, a few minutes later, came out dressed in dry clothes. She carefully hung her wet things on nails on the ceiling beam beside the stove. Her hair hung free.

He tried not to look at that delicate little piece of white lace hanging there. Did that mean she was no longer wearing a bra? He tried not to look at that either.

But he did. She had on another men's flannel shirt. Too large by three or four sizes. Knotted at the midriff. That one little knot made all the difference. Her belly button showed. It made his mouth go as dry as if he'd been stranded in a sandstorm. Impossible to tell if she was wearing a bra or not, though. The temptation was to soak her again and find out. He was lucky he was wearing these wet clothes. They deterred the fire that wanted to sputter to life inside of him.

She was getting a huge galvanized tub down from its peg on the wall.

"I'll take Rocky out into the sun," she said, gathering up the baby and the sleeping bag.

"Are you going to do my back?" he teased.

"Only with cat-o'-nines."

"Kinky," he said, wagging his eyebrows at her. He found out what a babe in the woods she really was when her face went from delicate pink to beet red in a breath. No smart retort, no quick comeback. She disappeared out the door as if the cabin had caught fire.

He contemplated that phrase. Babe in the woods. Rocky. Babe in the woods, beautiful woman. Babe in the woods, innocence. How did he get himself into these predicaments?

He reminded himself this wasn't a pleasure trip anyway. When she left the cabin, he forced himself to think business. He was guaranteed privacy for the next half hour or so. He stripped off his wet clothes and put them on the backs of chairs as close to the fire as he dared. And then, a towel knotted at his waist, he looked in all the drawers and every other nook and cranny for his gun. He moved dishes. He looked in the flour bag. He emptied the wood bin. He couldn't find it. He tried to think like she would think.

And thought of her taking him completely off guard by throwing her weight into the trough. He realized if he had a million years he was never going

to be able to think like she thought. He knew he'd
been a very, very sick man and that he was not yet
quite recovered because, suddenly, spending a million
years trying did not seem like it would be such a
terrible way to spend time.

Storm set the sleeping bag and Rocky in the clearing in front of the cabin. There was a coffee can on
the porch with wooden clothespins in it. She retrieved
it, snapped the lid on and brought it to the baby. She
rolled it for him to demonstrate the noise it made, and
he seemed very pleased with this primitive toy. The
sun was now out in full force and it promised to be
a glorious day.

The baby occupied, she pulled her brush out of her
back pocket and began to work furiously on the tan-
gles in her hair. It embarrassed her what she suddenly
wanted: a blow-dryer, a curling iron. A little pot of
eye shadow. She wanted to look pretty *for him*. Even
knotting her shirt had been about showing him she
could be feminine.

When they had laughed and played, she had felt so
wonderful, so alive, so exhilarated. Only, she tried to
tell herself, because she had experienced too many
shocks, too much stress the past few days.

When he had held her against his wet body, she
had felt something she had never, ever felt.

A deep awareness of herself as a woman.

It seemed to her she should have felt that with Dorian. But she had not really. She had felt flattered by
Dorian's attention. Swept away by it. She had for the
first time acknowledged the power her femininity had
given her over men.

Big deal. She could lure a married man away from

his wife. She was not sure she wanted that kind of power. And definitely not that kind of man.

But that awareness she had experimented with so briefly in Edmonton had not been like this. Core deep. Soul deep. That she was a woman. And wanted to be a woman. And wanted to experience everything a woman experienced.

Recipe for heartbreak, she told herself grimly. Maybe what she was feeling wasn't identical to what she had felt with Dorian, but close enough that she had better keep her guard up. She needed her wits about her to deal with Ben.

Oh, he was gorgeous, all right, and had her primal instincts humming.

But there was the deeper issue of trust here. And she knew she had better be careful.

As if to underscore that, she heard a drawer open inside the cabin, slide shut again. And then another one. She listened. Dishes rattled, and then the wood sounded as if it was being taken from the box one piece at a time. Then the box itself scraped across the floor.

He was looking for his gun.

Damn him. To go from a laughter-filled moment to looking for his gun.

Apparently not finding what he was looking for did not affect his temperament too adversely, because after a while she heard him whistling, heard the water being poured into the big galvanized tub. And then she heard him splashing. She ordered her mind not to go there. But it did anyway.

She thought of how it had felt to be pressed against him in her wet clothes, how much fun it had been to just let go with him, how natural it had felt to play together.

She realized she had not really let go like that for a long, long time.

She gave up on her hair, since it was impossible to see what ridiculous thing she had done to it without a mirror. She was hoping Shania, but suspected Madam Mim, so she pulled it back into her normal ponytail and pushed the coffee can around for Rocky.

Ben began to sing. "What do you do with a drunken sailor, what do you do with a drunken sailor—"

The baby turned toward the sound of his voice and smiled with such utter devotion it stole her heart. Then he gurgled loudly, almost as if he was trying to sing along.

Rocky seemed further delighted when she hummed and even more so when she picked up the chorus and sang along. She realized she would stand on her head and do back flips to earn his sweet little smile. When the time came, she added words, singing lustily, "Put him in the horse trough till he's sober, put him in the horse trough till he's sober."

"That's not how the song goes!" came an indignant voice from the other side of that cabin door.

"It is now," she informed him.

He was naked in there. In her cabin. In her bathtub. Just a few steps away. She could feel herself blushing at the thought.

"Shauna," she told herself, using the name that was her other half, the girl who was not nearly so wild and impetuous, so tough and strong as Storm, "you are a real babe in the woods sometimes."

She leveled a look at Rocky. "And don't you look so smug, because you are, too."

She lay back and contemplated the endless blue of the sky.

"This one's for you," Ben called. "I don't usually do dedications, but just this once, since you begged so nicely."

"I did not beg. I have never begged in my life."

"I could make you beg."

She had an awful vision of his lips. "You could not!"

"I have a very special recipe that would do it in a second."

That reminded her he had a life she knew nothing about. Probably just like a James Bond movie. Cooking gourmet meals for beautiful spies. He probably had a million women after him, especially when he relaxed, let the wall of steel down a little bit, like he was doing now.

"And what is that?" she called, pulling the baby onto her chest.

"Double-fudge sundaes, with whipping cream."

"Just sing," she said.

"I told you I could make you beg."

His voice, so wonderfully rich and deep when he spoke, did not really lend itself to song, not that that stopped him from a very robust version of "She'll Be Comin' Round the Mountain." Ridiculously, she decided she loved his singing.

She closed her eyes. He changed songs. And so, to the sound of "I had an old dog and his name was Caboo," she drifted off, not quite sleeping, enjoying the weight of the baby, his curious fingers tugging at her hair, probing her face and reaching in her ears.

She smelled it before she saw it. She lay perfectly still, though her arms tightened around Rocky. Carefully, she clicked open one eye.

A bear cub blinked at her.

It would have been too cute for words, except for one thing that every single person who spent any kind of time in the woods knew. Where there was a cub, there was a mother. And that mother had the most fierce maternal instinct ever put on this earth.

The bear cub, black fur sticking straight up just like Rocky's hair, sniffed his human counterpart with interest. Rocky regarded their visitor with wide-eyed delight, cooing greetings.

"Shoo," Storm croaked.

Out of the corner of her eye she saw the mama bear break the timber. In a move, faster than she would have thought she was capable of, Storm leaped to her feet, her arms wrapped around Rocky. It sent the bear cub tumbling.

He ran bawling toward his mother who regarded Storm with indignation. Mama Bear took a step toward them and rose on her hind legs, her teeth clicking in menace.

Storm was not a screamer. In fact, she had no patience at all with women who were, but she had no control over the sound of terror and panic that came right from her guts. She took poor Rocky by surprise, and he wailed.

The cabin door burst open, and Ben came out, a skimpy towel knotted at his waist. In a second he had the shotgun, which she knew wasn't loaded, and was running across the clearing, roaring at the bear.

The bear regarded him for a stunned moment, fell

back down on all fours, then turned and lumbered from the clearing, the cub at her heels.

Ben turned back to her. "Are you all right?"

"Yes." She studied him. His face was half-lathered and half-shaved. Beneath the lather he was ashen. She might have thought his half-shaved state was funny except for the strange beating of her heart. He was a man made to wear a loincloth. It showed off his every muscle, all of them corded with tension at the moment. "That shotgun's not loaded."

He looked at it, and then swore softly under his breath. "Is it always so bloody exciting around here?"

She could not take her eyes off him.

He seemed to realize he was not dressed. He looked down at himself, then looked up at her. He clutched his towel closer.

She raised an eyebrow at him. "Nice outfit," she said. "Kinky."

Then she brushed the tears from Rocky's cheeks, kissed him, turned and walked up the steps into the cabin.

Chapter Six

"Okay," he said, following her into the cabin and slamming the door behind him to make sure she knew he meant business. "No more Mister Nice Guy. Where's the gun?"

"You were never that nice a guy," she informed him.

He felt as if she'd kicked him. What about the lighthearted morning they had just spent together? He had serenaded her with his special rendition of "She'll Be Comin' Round the Mountain." Then again, maybe dumping her in the horse trough didn't exactly qualify him for the Mr. Universe of nice guys.

Still, it was that very kind of thing he had to be vigilant about. He'd let himself *play*, sing and behave most inappropriately. He'd forgotten, very nearly, that he was here to do a job. To keep that baby safe. And her too, now that she was involved.

He'd just gotten out of that ridiculous excuse for a tub and been shaving, using soap instead of shaving foam, which he hated, and trying to see in a mirror that had approximately the same reflective qualities as tinfoil, when he'd heard her scream.

His first thought had been that he'd done it again. Let his guard down, allowed himself to be lulled into a false sense of security. He'd burst out that door fully expecting to see the Crescada National Security Force—or at least some of their representatives—out there hurting his baby.

His baby. Even to think in those terms meant he had lost his objectivity somewhere along the way, that aloof distance he was able to maintain in most situations that gave him a cutting edge.

Because there had been no cutting edge in what he had just done. He'd actually been relieved it was a bear! He'd actually attacked the bear with nothing more than an unloaded shotgun.

His logic had completely abandoned him. He had been running on pure emotion since he had heard her scream. Something so primal in him that it had actually taken over. As he came out of that cabin door he had been full of pure feeling, and that feeling had been rage. He had heard the terror in her scream and had been enraged that anyone or anything could make her feel that way.

Even the bear had backed down from him. He suspected, uneasily, that the bear's legendary protective instincts did not hold a candle to his own when it came to that baby. *And her.*

Thank God he'd had the towel around his waist when it had happened. Otherwise, he would have been out there fighting off bears in the buff.

"The gun," he repeated coldly.

"No," she said, just like that.

He noticed she had put her hair in a ponytail that was already falling out, soft tendrils of hair framing a face that was lovely even with that stubborn set to it. He thought eyes the shade of hers should be declared illegal.

"I don't think you understand our situation here," he told her firmly.

"I don't think you do. You couldn't have killed that bear with a handgun. Wounded her. Made her really mad. I don't think you want to die looking like that, do you?"

She wasn't taking him seriously because he was in a towel! He realized his face was half shaven and half lathered with soap.

"I want that gun," he said in a no-nonsense tone of voice he usually reserved for when he did indoctrination sessions with recruits at the FIA training facility.

"I think your baby needs changing."

He glared at her. He could make full-grown men, hand-picked for their toughness and resiliency, tremble in their boots with that tone of voice.

And what did she mean *your baby?* He supposed his affection for that kid was right in his face for all the world to see, making her mistake him for some kind of softy.

"And so do you," she said cheerfully. She put the baby in his arms. And then moved by him. Just as she passed, before he knew what had happened, she reached out, slipped her fingers in between his waist and the towel and tugged. Hard.

The towel fell to the floor at his feet.

He whirled. She hadn't even turned back to look, just waltzed out the door, laughing.

To think, just this morning, he had rather enjoyed her laughter.

The baby smiled at him, gurgled.

"Oh, shut up," he said, deliberately using his boot-camp voice.

The baby laughed, reached up and grabbed a mitt full of his hair.

"That is not respectful!" What did he expect? Not even a baby could respect a man who had just been robbed of his towel, who now stood utterly naked, made mock of by a wee whip of a woman.

"Oooba dooba beb."

"Oh, right." For a man who knew he had to be hard, that the lives of three people might depend on it, he did not think he should be contemplating whether "beb" meant Ben.

Storm grabbed her slouch hat off the peg just inside the cabin door and went out. She went and lay back on the blanket. She put the hat over her face to keep the sun out of her eyes, but not before she saw him, baby in arms, peering out the window at her.

Was he still in the altogether? The thought should have made her smile, but instead her mouth felt strangely dry.

The truth was her final act of boldness had served a purpose. She hoped it made her seem somewhat worldly, as if she had a sophisticated sense of humor and had seen lots of men naked. Did he know she hadn't dared look once she had done the deed?

The deed had acted as a way of disguising from him how she really felt. Mortified by her own behavior. Out there screaming like a ninny. Never in her life had she screamed like that. She looked after things herself. She didn't rely on a man.

Good grief, it reminded her of her aunt Sally. Storm had personally watched her shoo a mouse out of her kitchen with a broom with complete calm one day when they had been alone together. A few days later the same woman had been standing on her kitchen chair screaming, while Uncle John ran around the kitchen valiantly trying to land a broom blow on the same mouse. It was almost as if her aunt had saved the mouse for this occasion!

Storm didn't understand those kind of games—or want to play them.

"It was a bear," she reminded herself in self-defense. "A little bigger than a mouse."

Still, the principle was the same. She had stood there helplessly and let him come to her rescue.

"You had the baby," she defended herself further. It was true, having the baby had made her think differently. Made her focus more on Rocky's safety than anything else, changed the fundamental way she dealt with things. Which was generally head-on.

Look at her, even now. Lying here on this blanket, as if she were a sunbathing queen. A woman of leisure. She had work to do. What was she waiting for? Ben's permission?

She had to take charge of her own life, and that was that. She got up and went back into the cabin.

He was fully dressed, though his clothes looked slightly damp, stiff and uncomfortable. She could offer him a clean, dry shirt but decided not to. Two could play "no more Mister Nice Guy—" or Nice Gal, as the case might be.

She also noticed both sides of his face were now

shaven. Without the rough stubble he could have looked like a businessman getting ready for work. Except for that alert and watchful light that never seemed to leave his eyes. His hair was drying to a lighter shade, just as she had guessed it would. Strands of honey-gold were mixed in liberally with the darker shades of brown.

He was clumsily dealing with the diaper. She could offer to help with that, too, but she wasn't going to.

She began shoving some crackers, cheese and dried meat into a little sack.

"You going somewhere?"

Okay, if she was really honest, she kind of missed Mister Nice Guy, who had serenaded her from the bathtub this morning, whose voice and eyes had shown a trace of human warmth for a few minutes.

He seemed as cold as ice now, as wary as when he had first showed himself at the edge of the clearing.

"I'm going to work on my riding trails," she said. "That's what I came here for."

"I'll come, too."

"Oh, really? To stand guard, or to be Mister Nice Guy again?"

"I thought I was never that nice a guy," he reminded her.

"Only when you want something. What do you want this time?"

"To keep you safe."

"Ha. And I suppose the gun would help with that?"

"Since you mention it, it would."

"There's no danger in these woods, Ben."

"That bear looked fairly hazardous to me."

"A situation I've handled dozens of times by myself. Dozens. Besides, I'll be using a chain saw. No self-respecting bear comes toward that kind of sound.''

"I'm not really worried about bears.''

She really hated it that he had the decency not to rub her face in the fact that for a woman who had handled that situation dozens of times, she had not exactly been handling it when he had burst out the door this morning.

"You see,'' he continued, "you can be wrong about danger. You can become comfortable in familiar surroundings and think nothing could ever happen there. I know. Because that's exactly how I felt the night Noel was shot.''

"Nobody's going to find that baby up here, Ben.''

"It's my job to act as though they could.''

"Fine. Come. Bring the baby. What do you know about chain saws?''

"Just what I saw in a particularly gruesome movie, once.''

They put the saw on the pack horse, Barney, along with a plastic container of gasoline. They would lead the horse. It would make it easier than getting on and off at every downed tree. It took an amazing amount of time to get a baby ready to go anywhere. Ben had looked over Rocky's blankets, soothers, food, formula and diapers, and had carefully selected items to meet any contingency. Even the teddy bear, the nice one with the chewed-off ear, was stuffed into a pillowcase to load on the horse.

"We'll start with the loop trail,'' she told him, when he was finally ready, the baby nestled happily in the crook of one of his strong arms.

One of her homemade signs marked the trailhead

just west of the cabin and she wished she could rip it down. The last thing she wanted to look like right now was a poet. Soft. Vulnerable. *Romantic*. She had called the trail Staircase to Heaven.

"It's a two-hour ride to a lookout," she said crisply. "It'll take us longer clearing. You'll understand why I call it that when you see it."

As it turned out, he handled the chain saw with ease. He handed her Rocky when they came to the first big hemlock down right across the trail. He bucked off the branches first.

"I don't think you learned everything you know about chain saws from a movie," she shouted over the idle of the chain-saw engine. She set the baby down on the blanket Ben had brought with him.

There, she'd caught him in another lie. Well, maybe not quite a lie, a fib. But the truth was, this man did not like to reveal things about himself at all. If he had not spent a day delirious, she would know nothing about him. Not one more thing than when he had first appeared at the edge of her clearing. None of the things that had made her reluctantly like him enough to relax with him this morning. Surely someone who gave a dog a name like Caboo could not be all bad.

"I guess I remember more from the ranch than I thought I did. It's been a long, long time since I handled one of these. Last time I was a boy, no bigger than you are now. I seem to remember it being quite a bit harder then. Isn't it hard for you?"

See? She shrieked at a bear, and the world branded her a weakling, and rightly so. Well, she'd show him. First she looked around for something to give Rocky to play with. Now that he'd had a close encounter with the real thing, he scoffed at the teddy bear. She finally found a baseball-sized rock, large enough that he couldn't squeeze it in his mouth, and set it on the blanket with him. He grunted mightily trying to pick it up.

Storm began to clear the branches, pouring on the energy. But the harder she worked, the harder it was to keep up to him. She wondered if the little edge of competitiveness between them had something to do with the tree being cleared off the trail in record time.

They worked hard, silently, the trail winding steadily upward. Of the three, only the baby seemed richly content, cooing and gurgling away to himself, playing with the rocks and cones she brought him, listening raptly to the sound of the saw, babbling to Barney.

They finally reached the lookout. Ben stood for a long time looking at the view, and when he turned back to her, some finely held tension seemed to have left him.

"You're right," he said.

"About not surrendering the gun?" she deadpanned, giving the baby a cracker to nibble on. She set the baby on the ground and sat down beside him, putting her back against the trunk of a tree.

"About the view! It does seem to be about as close to heaven as a man could get on this earth." Did his eyes really trail briefly to her lips and then skitter away?

Did hers really go to his?

"This is where I have a lunch break with my trail riders," she said, looking for anything to fill the sudden electric silence between them.

"They must love it." He came and sat beside her.

He had packed everything but the kitchen sink for the baby and had no lunch for himself. She passed him her lunch bag and he helped himself to some jerky.

She thought it was unfortunate that he had used the word *love,* though she couldn't really say why. Maybe because it seemed, suddenly, like *love* should be a word reserved for bigger things than mere enjoyment. "I've had people come from all over the world. Japan. Greece. Africa."

"What got you into this?"

"I wanted to be up here. I wanted to make a living. I help on the ranch, but I wanted to have something that was all mine, so I didn't feel as if I was dependent on my brothers. I'm going to buy my own ranch someday." She said this with a touch of defiance, since the few people she had shared that idea with seemed to think it was beyond her reach.

"I don't doubt it for a minute."

She stared hard at him.

"I mean it. There are people in this world who want to do and people who do. You're a doer. If you can run this business, I'm sure a ranch would be child's play for you. This is tough work for a person to take on alone. You do it alone, right?"

"Yes. Sometimes I drive my brothers crazy. They want to help and I won't let them. They worry."

"I can understand that. I think I'm glad I'm not your brother."

That made her face go all hot because that could be taken two ways. And when she looked at his lips again, she felt glad he was not her brother, too.

"And what about this little spread you dream about? Are you going to do that by yourself, too?"

"I hope to. I've taken some agricultural courses at university."

"Somehow I can't see you at university. Scare the hell out of those academic boys."

"I didn't finish. I hated the city."

"Which city?"

"Edmonton." She tried to keep the pain out of her voice, but she could see from the way he looked at her so intently he heard something.

"You know, Storm, most people dream their dreams with other people."

"I'm not most people."

"You can't let that SOB who hurt you steal your whole life from you."

"He doesn't have anything to do with this!"

"I see in your eyes how much he has to do with this. Independent woman, can do it all alone, never going to be burned again."

"I thought you were a secret agent. Not a psychiatrist. Who are you to talk, anyway? You seem to go it alone, too. Or is there a woman tucked away somewhere waiting for you?" Why had her heart stopped beating, waiting for his answer?

"No," he said, slowly. "This lifestyle isn't compatible with relationships."

Her heart started beating again. "Neither is this one."

"Storm, don't choose my way. Someday you'll look back and be sorry."

"Are you?"

He was silent and looked out over the view. When he looked back, she saw the answer in his eyes, a loneliness that seemed to go soul deep. It was gone quickly, masked.

"Who burned you?" she asked boldly.

"I didn't get burned," he said. "I just faced up to facts, early. Men have all these neat little compartments for their lives. One for work, one for sports, one for travel, one for relationships. Are you following?"

She nodded.

"For men, a relationship fits neatly into one of those compartments. It's not his whole life. A woman wants to make a relationship everything. It's the biggest compartment in her life, and then she wants to somehow get it into all the other compartments, too."

"That's a chauvinist thing to say," she said.

"That's probably a hanging offense up here on Storm Mountain, hmm? Being a chauvinist?"

"Nah. Just forty lashes."

"Don't get into the cat-o'-nine stuff again, Storm." He looked at her and grinned with wicked satisfaction. "You're blushing!"

"I am not!"

"I bet you didn't even look when you grabbed the towel!"

Now how should she answer that? Did too? What if he had a birthmark?

"So you don't have a girlfriend," she said, "and you don't have a wife. How could you possibly be any kind of expert on women, clingy or otherwise?"

"I'm expert enough to know you're innocent," he said softly. "Ooh, now you're really blushing. Didn't you and that married guy—"

"None of your cotton-pickin' business!"

"You're right. It isn't."

"Do you just ask personal questions and never answer any? Is that it?"

"Ask me anything. Really personal."

"I already did. Who burned you?"

"I thought I told you my life history in fevered bits and pieces."

"Betty-Lou?" she guessed.

"No."

There. But just when she decided he was being true to form and would never reveal anything about himself without force or delirium, he said softly, "My parents made me wary of relationships. Match made in hell. Immature city girl marries simple rancher. She made him her whole life, but then she wanted him to do the same thing. She couldn't believe things came before her. Things like feeding cattle, riding range, branding. She blamed him for her unhappiness for seventeen years, then she left him."

"I'm sorry."

"He was a good man. He really tried. Anyway, I was only sixteen when the big bust up happened, and she wanted me to go with her. And my dad thought I should, too. I think he wanted me to look after her. I didn't do any better at it than he had. I guess by then unhappiness had become a habit with her. Because she was still unhappy when she left him."

Storm was shocked at how much of himself he'd revealed. By the look on his face, he was already regretting it.

"It wasn't that it was a habit with her," Storm said softly. "It's that she looked in all the wrong places for happiness. I found that out from Dorian."

"Dorian?"

"The snake."

"Oh, him. The *married* snake."

"People don't make each other happy. They find

happiness inside themselves first, and then they give that, like a gift, to the person they decide to have a relationship with.''

"Storm?''

"Huh?''

"The next guy you decide to have a relationship with is going to be one lucky man.''

"Oh, I don't think I'll go rushing into anything.''

"How long has it been?''

"Two years.''

"I'd say you're not rushing things! Two years of grieving and hiding and beating yourself up and *nothing* happened between you?''

"Something happened. It just wasn't sex!''

"What was it then?''

"I was betrayed.''

"You made a mistake and you can't forgive yourself.''

She didn't look at him. "Maybe,'' she finally admitted.

"Don't the guys from around here beat a path to your door?''

"First they have to get past my brothers glaring at them. After I beat them at arm wrestling, they're about as scared of me as those college boys were. Men are easily threatened.''

"That's a generalization.''

"And 'all women seek their ultimate happiness in a man' was not?''

"I think you're hiding up here,'' he told her quietly.

Actually, she had wondered that herself. If she was hiding from life and all its hurts up here in her mountains. Up here she was in control, or had been until the moment he'd appeared.

But now, looking at him, she wondered. She wondered if she'd been hiding at all. Maybe healing would have been a better word.

Maybe even waiting.

Though her first temptation was just to deny she was hiding, to really hide in some snappy one-line comebacks, she took a small chance. And told him how she really felt.

"Maybe," she said slowly, "when I'm up here, I'm working on the happy part. Because this—" she swung her arm around at the panoramic view "—makes me happy. Really happy, the way-down-deep-inside kind."

He looked at her, and then looked around. "I guess it makes me feel that way, too. Not giddy happy. Quiet happy. Contented. Full."

"There's only one other thing that seems to make me feel the way this place makes me feel," she said, uncertain how much she should tell him, uncertain how far she wanted this honesty to go.

"What's that?"

She nodded at the baby. "Him."

He looked at the baby and smiled with reluctant tenderness. "He has a way of making me feel things, too."

And then he looked at her, taking her by complete surprise.

Because he leaned toward her and kissed her right on the lips. Softly, tenderly, with a fire burning just below the surface. He broke away before she did, but not before she felt the pull of him, stronger than the pull of the tide toward the moon.

She stared at him wide-eyed. She touched her lips.
"Why did you do that?"

"I'm not quite sure. Maybe I wanted to you to feel
something."

"Like what?"

"Everything you're missing."

"And what did you feel?" she stammered.

"A little bit of your happiness, I think. That down-
deep-inside kind."

But if he had felt it, he had also taken some of it
away with him, because when she stood up quickly
and brushed off the crumbs, it wasn't happiness she
was feeling.

But a sensation of being deeply disturbed, confused, on the verge of discovery and on the verge of
tears.

He looked at her. "I'm sorry," he said. "I
shouldn't have done that."

Which, of course, only made everything worse.

"No," she agreed tartly. "You shouldn't have."

"Ooba dooba beb," the baby shouted.

Storm looked at him absently. "It sounds as if he's
trying to say Ben," she said.

Chapter Seven

He'd kissed her. The sweat ran off him in rivulets as he took out his fury at himself on a huge lodgepole pine that was down across the trail. He refused the chain saw, hacking the branches off with an ax instead.

Whack. Whack. Whack.

Keep his distance. Keep his cool. Keep his edge. That had been the plan.

And then she'd taken him to the top of the world, walked him right up her own staircase to heaven, and he didn't know what had gotten into him.

First he'd told her about his dysfunctional family, a subject he had managed to remain silent on, even during a time when it had been somewhat fashionable to discuss these matters. The agency had a shrink on staff, and a once-a-year session with him was mandatory, just like having a physical. He'd stonewalled the good doctor, a man trained to suck secrets out of people, with absolute ease. In fact, he seemed to recall he'd made the little runt quite mad by calling him Dr. Brainpicker instead of Dr. Pickleblain. For the past several years the doctor handed him a *Sports Illustrated* and hid behind his paperwork while Ben contentedly caught up on his reading.

Was there another living soul on earth, outside of the parties who'd been involved in that miserable union, who knew about it, who needed to know about his family?

What in her eyes had beckoned to that vulnerable place inside of him, told him if he spoke of it, it would be gone, laid to rest, that he would be left more free to choose a different path? What path would he choose?

Whack. Whack. Whack.

Get a grip, McKinnon. It was not as if he was a teenager, free to start rethinking his career. Though lots of guys retired young from this kind of work.

So, just what if? What if he was free to choose again?

It occurred to him he had liked everything about the ranch, the animals, the hard work, the clean air, but he had never been able to separate his love for it from the pain his parents' constant bickering had brought him.

Whack. Whack. Whack.

Pickleblain would love this kind of introspection.

He tried to focus on cleanly severing the branches from the trunk, but all his might seemed incapable of turning off his mind, and now it wandered to her.

As if it had not been enough to lay his soul at her feet, then he had thought he had caught a glimpse of hers. And felt compelled to fix something in her that would have been better left alone.

It had become apparent to him that she was planning on spending her life as a celibate because of some married snake that she'd had the good sense not to give in to. Which left him uncomfortably contemplating something that was really none of his business. *Really*.

Was she a virgin? He nearly chopped off his thumb.

Still, for the strangest moment, as he stood there regarding his thumb, it seemed like that was why he was here, how he had found his way across the world to her. That it had nothing to do with the baby, that Rocky had just been the vehicle that had brought him to this place in his destiny.

All the world, all the circumstances of that puzzling world, seemed to have led him to this spot.

Him and her, sitting at the edge of heaven.

That view could be described as nothing less than heavenly: blue-ridged mountains rolled away into eternity; smoky green forests climbed mountain walls; secretive treed valleys offered glimpses of small lakes the color of jewels, jade, turquoise and olive. The view was magnificent, about as close as a man could get on this earth to heaven.

Or so he'd convinced himself until the exact moment that he'd tasted her lips.

Heaven had redefined itself at warp speed.

He had convinced himself that kissing her was just the right thing to do. A good deed, right up there with the sweet Boy Scout walking the little old lady across the road. Altruistically, Ben had decided to show her what she was missing. Release her from her prison. Let her know passion was one of the wonders of the world, that it rated even higher than this lofty view she had brought him to see.

He hadn't quite thought far enough ahead to know what he was going to do with all that passion if he did manage to break the chains around it, coax it out.

Coax it! It had leaped off her lips to his.

She was practically on fire, that girl. No wonder. Two years? Without so much as a kiss?

Of course, if the amount of time spent in abstinence was the measuring stick, he'd be pretty near the ignition point himself.

This situation now had danger coming from angles he had never had to deal with before. Danger outside himself, maybe. Danger inside himself, definitely.

He cursed out loud. And she looked up.

She was sweating, too, her hair damp from it, curling around her face where it had worked free of the ponytail. Little diamond beads of perspiration were on her brow and above the fullness of lips, which looked glossy, like she had just licked them. He was not sure that he had ever seen a woman work like this, so comfortable with her physical self.

What exactly might that translate to on other playing fields?

If he ever found out, if he took it anywhere, if he allowed it to go anywhere, he'd be as bad as the snake. Worse.

He nearly moaned out loud when he thought about that cabin. What was he going to do tonight? Sleep on the porch?

Now he had the right idea. Do his job. Stand guard. Sleep on the porch.

He wondered if life could really get much more unfair. He was on fire for a woman he was sworn to protect, and now protecting her had another dimension. Her own innocence needed protecting from *him*. It was a twist to the tale that he didn't like one bit. He was a man accustomed to control.

She paused and took off the flannel shirt. Underneath it she was wearing a T-shirt. An ordinary white T-shirt that had Williams Lake Stampede emblazoned across the front of it.

But with just the smallest effort he could make out the white outline of her bra through the thin, sweat-dampened cotton of the shirt. He suspected, in the brief glance he allowed himself before he looked away, that it was a frilly one just like that one hanging on the nail above the stove.

What did that mean? That under those boyish clothes she wore things so delicately feminine?

Okay, God, he thought, I get it. It can get more unfair. So please don't turn up the bloody heat anymore.

"Beb, beb, beb, beb," the baby cried.

When Ben turned and looked at him, Rocky stopped shouting and grinned his most endearing toothless grin. When he turned away again the boisterous shouting resumed, until he turned around. More grins. Jeez, if the kid wasn't trying to talk to him!

He set down the ax he'd been using to hack off branches and picked up the baby. He put him at arm's length above his head, and Rocky wagged his legs and arms, chuckling happily.

"Beb, beb!"

He glanced down the trail, where Storm was throwing logs he had cut up off the trail with strength and energy that was going to outlast his. Didn't she know he was just getting over being ill? No doubt that also explained this unnatural vulnerability he was feeling. This unmanly tendency to reveal things about himself. This undisciplined longing to taste her lips once more. Twice more. Maybe more than twice more.

"Beb, beb!"

"That's right," he said softly. "Me Beb-beb."

What the hell? If he was getting soft, he might as well do it thoroughly. He could blame his depleted resources. He kissed the baby on the end of his little button nose before he set him down.

"Hey, Beb-beb."

Ben turned and glared at Storm. He hoped to hell she hadn't witnessed him kissing the baby.

"I think we better head down. You've probably had enough for one day."

Actually, he hadn't. If they worked much longer, he could go back to the cabin, lie on the porch and die. Which seemed infinitely preferable to lying on the porch thinking about her lips.

At least the weather was warmer than it had been. He should be able to keep from freezing on the porch tonight. And tomorrow they could come out here and work themselves to exhaustion again, work right past the desire that burned in their eyes with every glance, with every casual touch.

"I'm okay, if you want to finish," he called to her.

Storm came back to him. She wiped sweat from her brow and took a deep swig of water, which made him look again at her lips.

"We better go," she said. "There's bad weather brewing."

He looked at the clear sky and back at her. Was

she trying to give him an excuse to quit that wouldn't injure his pride?

"Trust me on this one," she said.

"It's gorgeous out here."

Gorgeous. A funny word to describe the weather. But it was how she looked *exactly*.

"I know, but the weather in these mountains can change in a blink. Didn't you feel the wind change? There's a funny heat in it. I'm sure something's coming."

Oh, he felt the wind change, all right. The wind had changed, blowing hot as a Sierra breeze, the minute he had put his fool lips to hers. Lips as soft as the petals of a flower, lips that had the most enticing polarity, white-as-snow innocence and red-as-coal desire both there in equal measure.

She glanced at the sky again and said, "I think we'd better hurry. I don't want Rocky to get wet."

He glanced at the sky and saw nothing. Blue skies. Big white clouds. Still, it would be okay to quit for Rocky's benefit, if not his own.

But within five minutes Ben had tucked the baby right inside his own shirt to try and protect him from a wind growing in intensity by the second.

By the time they were back at the cabin, the wind was howling and the sky was black. The quiet horse was rolling his eyes and snorting. Hard raindrops had started to fall. The baby liked it inside his shirt, cooing softly and pulling on his chest hairs.

The wind was blowing the rain right up under the porch.

And he knew he wasn't spending the night outside.

That, despite his specific request, the heat was going to be turned up tonight. Big time.

Storm liked being in the cabin when the rain pounded on the shake roof and the wind screamed around the corners and under the eaves. Inside, the fire crackled, the lantern sent a circle of golden light out from the table, and supper cooking smelled good. Usually, in these circumstances she would have felt cozy and safe.

But tonight, she felt strangely edgy, as if something building inside her put the fury and wrath of that outer storm to shame.

Not wanting to contemplate that too long, almost afraid it would take on a life of its own if she gave it her energy, she checked her dumplings, floating like clouds in the stew gravy, and then added some canned peaches to the cobbler she was making.

She looked over at Ben and felt a stab of guilt. She had pushed him too hard after his being so sick. He had appeared so strong, so robust, it was easy to forget he had been ill. He looked done in, though manfully tried not to show it. In fact, he had the big ax between his knees and was filing the edges on it.

She stole a single look at his lips. How could anything that looked so hard, so stern be so soft, so tender?

She mashed up some of the stew and dumplings for the baby. She felt he should be thrilled by this change from peas but when she brought over a little bowl, Rocky wouldn't eat.

"Beb-beb," he called, frantically waving at Ben.

"Okay, give the Beb-beb stuff a rest, junior." He took the bowl from her and aimed the spoon at Rocky's mouth. Rocky pouted, his mouth turned down and his brows furrowed dramatically.

"Not in front of people," Ben ordered tersely.

"He can't understand you!" she said. "Not *what* in front of people?"

"Oh, he likes me to play a stupid little game with him."

"Really?"

"Kind of persuade him to eat."

"Well, don't be shy now. You sang to me today. Lost your towel. The time for embarrassment between us is over."

"Oh, I'm so glad to hear that," he said sarcastically. "Maybe later tonight we can play strip poker."

He had made his point, because she was still very capable of being embarrassed around him. She tried not to let it show, though. It would not do to let Ben get the upper hand.

"Open up." He growled the command at the baby.

Rocky pinched his lips together.

Ben sighed. "Chugga-chugga choo-choo."

She glanced over, trying not to laugh out loud. Magically the little mouth opened. The baby's eyes widened as he tasted the stew. He pounded a chubby fist on the table, and no more train noises were required to make him open his mouth.

She felt smug. Not only was she ruggedly independent, she could cook up a storm.

And why was it so important that Ben know that?

Oh, she hadn't just cooked up a storm. One was brewing. Even if she tried to ignore it, it was right there, on the horizon, black clouds building, the wind picking up heat, speed and intensity.

The baby finished his stew, and Ben tasted some from the bowl he put in front of him. His eyes closed with pleasure, and then he looked at her.

"Is there anything you can't do?" he asked.

"I don't know," she said. "There's a few things I haven't tried yet."

And they both knew what one of them was, and that it was going to be a long and feverish night in that cabin dealing with storms.

The baby fell asleep in Ben's arms almost immediately after he'd eaten. Ben held him for a while, enjoying the softness of him, the smell of him, the steady rise and fall of his little chest, more than he wanted to. Really, these sensations he was feeling, of tenderness, of connection, were making him feel like a stranger to himself.

Dr. Pickleblain would probably have a field day inside his head right now. With that thought in mind, he went and laid Rocky on the mattress and covered him with their one and only sleeping bag.

The silence, the flickering fire, the golden light of the lantern—the way it caught in the blackness of her hair and reflected softly off the perfection of her skin—were going to make him do something he regretted again, he was sure of it.

"Have you got a deck of cards?" he blurted out. He'd play a few hands of solitaire. It was a game he was good at, which he used often to disengage his mind from a stressful situation.

"You play poker?" she asked.

He raised an eyebrow at her.

"I didn't say strip poker!" she told him flatly, folding her arms over her chest.

"I've played. A little," he said cautiously. As if cards were not a way of life for men who often found themselves a long way from home with no place to spend their money.

"You want to have a few hands?"

"You play poker?" Why would that surprise him? She arm wrestled, wrangled horses, cleared brush, all like a man.

"Are you kidding? Two brothers, long winter nights. I own half the cattle on our ranch, six horses and a pig because of it."

He dealt. The cards were a mess, stained and dog-eared.

After four or five hands he was playing with a marked deck, even if she wasn't. Ace of diamonds, coffee stain, dime-sized, dead center. Ace of spades, torn. Ace of hearts, dog-eared, left corner.

She didn't play poker like a man. Even without being able to read more than half the deck, which he could, he could tell when she was delighted and when she was disappointed with the cards she had been dealt. It occurred to him that he could tell that even though her features were schooled into careful stillness.

How was it possible to feel he knew her so well in such a short time?

He decided to raise the stakes. He wouldn't play for the gun right away. He'd let her win a few hands first. The problem was he didn't have much to gamble with.

"Want to play for something?" he asked, ever so casually, after he'd allowed her quite a winning streak.

"Like what?" she said.

"You have a fairly nice horse."

"As far as I can see, all you have is a baby to ante up with, and I don't want him."

"Why not? I thought you were getting kind of attached to the little feller."

"All he does is eat, sleep and poop." The words did not disguise her affection for Rocky in the least.

"That's all your horse does, too!"

"My horse is not on the table."

"Well, ma'am," he drawled, "I can see there's no horse on the table. I doubt if this table would hold a horse."

She laughed, giggled like a schoolgirl.

Which should serve nicely to remind him that's really all she was. A schoolgirl. A babe in the woods.

He was not allowed to be the big, bad wolf. Well, maybe long enough to get the gun.

"You could throw in your hat," he suggested. "I've taken a liking to it."

"And what will you throw in? Not the baby."

"Three disposable diapers?" he said, hopefully.

"They don't even make good fire starter. Besides, you need them."

"I've got twenty bucks in my wallet."

"American?"

"Yeah."

"Now you're talking."

He let her win. And then they went again. She bet her hat, he his pocketknife. He was sorry to give her the knife. His old man had given it to him for his fourteenth birthday. For some reason, though, if he had to lose it, he was glad he had lost it to her.

"I've got a slightly used passport we could go for," he said.

"Ha. Which one?"

"Which one did you like the best?"

"None of them. Besides, what good is a man's passport to me?"

"You'd be amazed what you can do with disguises."

"Oh, another area you're an expert in."

He could see bringing up those passports had made her touchy, a small tactical error on his part, so he changed direction. "How about a pair of new baby shoes? Adidas."

He'd bought those at the store along with the baby food and diapers. Rocky refused to keep them on his feet.

"Baby shoes? I don't need baby shoes."

"Come on. They'd look cute hanging from your truck mirror."

"I've already got my lucky rabbit's foot hanging from my truck mirror."

"Okay. How about a teddy bear?"

"Have you got a gambling problem? You'd gamble with your kid's teddy bear? Of course, I'm not taking his teddy bear."

Your kid. There it was again. "What makes you think you'd win?"

"History?"

"I know. I'll trim your horse's feet."

"You know how?"

"Sure. A man doesn't forget that kind of thing." Oddly, though, he had managed to forget. For years he had not thought about the deep pleasure he had always felt when he worked with the ranch horses, rode out after cattle. Now his awareness seemed to be with him all the time, like an ache.

"I don't know. I usually don't trust my horse's feet to just anyone."

"How can you call me just anyone? After this morning? We had a bath together." He watched her face catch fire. It was a very becoming shade of red, he thought, though it was another strong reminder of what he was dealing with here. Innocence.

"Deal the cards," she sputtered.

He let her win again. And again. Until she was beaming with confidence.

"Want to go for the gun?" he asked casually.

"I already have the gun!" she pointed out.

"If you win, I won't ask for it again."

He knew she wouldn't be able to resist. She thought she was on a winning streak. And he was right, she wasn't able to. It was reassuring that he was still able to read people, especially a person with whom he had lost his impartiality.

But halfway through that hand, she dropped her cards, face up, on the table.

"You SOB," she said softly.

"Pardon?"

"You're cheating!"

"If I was cheating, don't you think I'd be winning?"

"You're manipulating me." She turned her cards over and studied the fronts of them. "Oh, I get it. This coffee stain means something to you, doesn't it?"

"Maybe."

"Tell me you weren't cheating."

He wasn't quite the man he used to be, because he found himself unable to lie to her, even though this would definitely fall into the category of a necessary lie.

"It's not exactly cheating," he said carefully. "It's

not my fault your cards all have personalities of their own. You should really think about investing in a new deck of cards.''

"I don't generally have sharpies on my rides.''

"Well, you should protect yourself against that eventuality.''

"You let me win! Just so you could get that stupid gun.''

"Does this mean I can have my knife back?''

"I'm keeping the knife and everything else, you...you...despot!''

"Despot? I think that's a little strong.''

"Really?'' She shoved back her chair and got up. "You're not just a liar. You're a cheat, too.''

"That's pretty strong, too. You know, if your deck of cards at the ranch looks anything like this, I could show you how to improve your holdings in that herd.''

He decided it was probably a good thing she didn't have the gun in her hand. She'd probably be shooting holes in the floor in front of him, saying, "Dance, you varmint.''

"You'd show me how to cheat my brothers?''

"Storm! I was kidding.''

"Kidding? You probably find it really amusing being up here with a naive little country mouse.''

"Mouse?'' he sputtered. "You?''

She continued as though she hadn't heard him. "You probably find it very amusing taking advantage of me with your slick ways.''

"You don't even know what taking advantage means,'' he warned her in a growl.

"Nothing about you is true, is it? Everything you do is contrived. Even when you make me laugh, it's only to get my guard down, only because you want something.''

He knew exactly what was happening, but he sure didn't want to be the one to point it out to her. Unfortunately, there was no one else here.

''Are you talking to me, Storm, or your friend Dorian?'' he asked quietly.

The truth of it hit her square between the eyes, and for a moment she looked shocked, as if she was going to crumple like a child whose dog had died. Then she drew herself to her full height, which was not that much, though she still managed to look as regal as a queen.

''There's more than one variety of snake,'' she said. ''And I seem to have a talent for attracting them all.''

She blew out the lantern, he suspected so he could not read her face, and then in the dim light he saw her go and slip under the blanket beside Rocky. ''And don't think you're sleeping here,'' she said.

''Who would want to?'' he shot back. ''It would be more pleasant to sleep with a porcupine. And to take advantage of one, too.''

She sniffed with contempt but did not respond, except to pull the baby in a little closer to her. As if the baby needed protecting from the big, bad wolf, too.

He contemplated her shape, a lump under the sleeping bag, for a full minute before he allowed himself to see the irony. He'd expected it was going to be hot as the Fourth of July in here tonight, maybe even hoped, way down deep in his secret self, for a few fireworks.

And instead the chill rolling off her was enough to freeze the water to ice right in the buckets.

A good reminder, he told himself, curling up on one of the bunks with her jacket, that nothing but nothing ever went the way you thought it was going to go with a woman.

Chapter Eight

It was cold in the cabin when Storm woke up in the morning. She wouldn't be surprised to see ice in the water buckets. She made sure the sleeping bag was tucked in tight around the baby, then glanced over at the bunk.

Empty.

Ben came in from outside and shook himself. His arms were full of wood. "There's snow out there. Lots of it."

Storm didn't respond. She was still mad at him, after all, and wanted him to know it.

"It's June for Pete's sake!" He dumped the wood at the firebox.

"You're in the high country." Every word came out clipped. "It's not that unusual at this time of year. It won't last. It'll be gone in an hour or two."

"Really? Wake up the baby!"

"What? Why?"

"He's never seen snow before. He may never see

it again." He came over in two quick strides and yanked down the covers.

"Hey!"

But he was ever so gentle as he picked up the sleeping baby, then blew on his eyelashes to make him wake up.

The baby scrunched up his eyes.

Ben blew again.

The baby opened them, cooed softly. It sounded like he said "Beb-beb."

Ben chuckled and tickled the baby under his chin.

It really bugged her that he could, in odd and scattered moments, look as if he was such a good man. A manipulative liar and cheat in one blink, a tender and loving daddy-type in the next.

Or was it possible he was correct? She looked at him, and the pain and betrayal that Dorian had caused overshadowed her seeing what he really was? Caused her to look at the whole world with suspicion now?

He deserved her suspicion, she told herself. All he wanted was that gun.

But then maybe he really did have a good reason for wanting the gun. Maybe if she'd done the kind of work he had done for as long as he had done it, she would want a gun, too, would start to feel as if it was a part of her. Feel naked without it.

Not that she wanted to start thinking naked thoughts. She sat up abruptly, ran her fingers through her tangled hair. Her elastic band had broken during the night, and her hair was all over the place. Why would she still care if her hair looked good? Which it didn't. Couldn't.

She wondered if, given time, she would ever unlock the secrets of him.

But that was something, thankfully, she would never know. Because they had no time. A week in the grand scheme of things was a fairly minuscule measure. She thought back. This was day four. Which meant that at the most, she had four days left with Ben and the baby. Four days unless Ben planned to leave in the morning of the seventh day.

Had he meant a week *exactly*, or a week *approximately?* Could she ask him? Ask him what time he planned to leave?

Or would it be obvious that she was counting hours then?

With dread.

How could she not want him to go? Last night she would have liked to hit him over the head with her best cast-iron frying pan.

She told herself, grimly, it was the baby.

She looked at Ben again, and could not help but smile, because with Rocky, it seemed he had no secrets at all. Everything that he was showed in the unguarded tenderness in his features right now as the baby came awake completely and made a wild grab for his nose.

"You want to see some snow, Rocky? White stuff? Cold?"

"Ben?" she asked.

He turned his attention from the baby and looked at her.

"Why might he never have a chance to see snow again?"

He looked swiftly away from her.

"What's going to happen to him? To Rocky? When all this is over? In four days?" She snuck in the time question to see if he would confirm or deny it. Strangely, the one thing she did not have one single doubt about was Ben's ability to keep this child safe. Not one.

"I don't know."

"You must have some idea." Was he being evasive? Just when she was beginning to feel as if maybe, just maybe, she could trust him? "Will you have to take him back to that place? What did you say it was called? Crescada?"

"Storm, I just don't know."

"Can't you keep him?"

He looked back at her then, his expression incredulous. "Keep him? I'm a single guy. I live out of a duffel bag. I travel around the world. Keep him?"

"I know it seems ridiculous—"

"Yes, it does!"

"—but he likes you so much."

"He likes me? How would you know that? Did he tell you?"

"Maybe not in words. But I can see it in the way he looks at you, waves his arms around when he sees you, calls you Beb-beb and won't eat for anybody else."

"I don't think that means he likes me, necessarily."

"Oh? And what do you think it means?"

"How do I know?" Ben's tone was becoming quite defensive. "For all I know Beb-beb means 'I have gas.'"

"You know what it means," she said quietly.

He was silent.

"You know what it means," she repeated.

"Okay. Maybe it does mean he likes me. You can't just keep a baby because he likes you."

"Does he have relatives then? In Crescada?"

He seemed to be very interested in the baby's fingernails. "No. Noel told me they were on their own."

"So will he stay here? Go back there? He won't—" she had to bite her tongue for a minute to keep her voice from trembling "—he won't go to an orphanage, will he?"

"I don't know!" He did not want to be pressed on this issue.

"It would be a shame if a stranger adopted him, when somebody already loves him so much."

"Who loves him?"

Me. "You."

"I don't *love* him, exactly."

She could tell he was terrified of that word. A man who attacked a bear with an unloaded shotgun and a towel. "How do you feel *exactly?*"

"I don't know." He was beginning to look impatient, brows drawing down over eyes that she could see pain in. Maybe he did not have as many secrets as he thought. Except from himself.

"Do you know how many times you have said 'I don't know' in the last sixty seconds?"

"I wasn't counting."

"Six. That's a lot of 'I don't knows.'"

He glared at her.

"Maybe," she suggested, getting up and moving by him, "you need to start thinking about all those things you don't know about."

She yanked open a drawer in search of a band for her hair. She was aware her clothes were wrinkled beyond belief. She couldn't find an elastic to pull her hair back with. Her hand went to her hair.

"A mess," he told her, coldly, just to let her know

their previous discussion had not gotten under his skin.

"Madam Mim," she agreed, with a sigh.

"Who?"

"The little fat witch in *The Sword and the Stone*, the Disney version."

He looked at her and sighed. "More like Shania," he muttered, then turned to the baby. "Hey, big guy, what do you want for breakfast. Bacon? Eggs? Belgian waffles?"

"Pancakes," she said, knowing what ingredients she had.

"I was getting to that." He consulted with Rocky, lowered his ear to the baby's lips. "He agrees to pancakes. Who wouldn't, after a few days of instant peas?" The baby gurgled. "Lots of syrup? I'm with you, bud. So, pancakes it is, and then we'll get out in that snow before it melts."

"I didn't see a snowsuit in that pack."

"Well, if you didn't see it after all the rummaging you've done in that pack, then I guess it wasn't there."

"Are you insinuating I'm a snoop?"

"Insinuating nothing. You know the contents of that pack better than I do." He ignited the kindling, and soon the stove was roaring.

She watched him cook, while she tried to get the knots out of her hair. Shania. Ha ha.

He scorched the pancakes slightly, a fact that did not perturb Rocky in the least, probably because of the generous amount of syrup Ben poured over them. She was sorry he didn't have to do the choo-choo train. Her hair was mostly tamed, though still no elastic. She joined them.

"Snowsuit?" Storm asked him.

"I'll be creative. You should wear your hair like that all the time."

"Right. Let's have Halloween all year long."

"What does that mean?"

"My hair looks like a witch's wig."

"No," he said, "it doesn't."

She could not stand the intensity of his gaze, could not meet his eyes without thinking of his lips. "So," she said, looking everywhere but at him, "speaking of witches—"

"Which I wasn't," he reminded her.

"—how are you going to conjure up a snowsuit?"

After breakfast, Ben showed her. He shoved the baby into three pairs of sleepers. The snaps were nearly bursting off the last pair as he did them up, and Rocky was beginning to sweat and protest. Then Ben snipped a small poncho out of a plastic bag, tying it securely at Rocky's waist with a piece of binder twine. He put tiny socks on Rocky's hands for mittens and jammed his feet into those little Adidas shoes, then cut out more of the garbage bag to wrap around each shoe.

"He looks like an elf," Storm decided. "From a bargain store."

"Well, bring on Santa and the reindeer. We're ready." Ben grinned at her, then scooped up the baby in his arms.

She did not want to be sucked into this.

She wanted to once again be the woman who believed this man was a world-class liar, cheat and manipulator.

But she could not resist him. Not when he was like

this. Full of energy and playfulness, so totally focused on bringing that baby some joy.

He did not have a jacket, himself, or mittens, but that didn't stop him.

She pulled her own jacket off the hook and followed them outside. She registered the look of astonishment on the baby's face when he saw the snow and registered the look of enjoyment on Ben's.

Ben reached down and scooped up a handful of the wet snow and threw it at her.

Don't play with him, she ordered herself. She told herself he was probably just after the gun again. She told herself it was just going to hurt more when they left if she allowed herself to be drawn into this.

When they left.

In four days. Maybe not even four whole days.

That's what she had to remind herself. The fact that he had this other personality, daddy of the year, should really just prove to her he could shed his skin as easily as a snake. He was leaving. And he was taking that baby with him. The baby's future was uncertain.

And so, she suspected, was his. He could be half a world away by next Monday. In some country she had never heard of, using a name she would never recognize.

He set Rocky in the snow. The baby reached out with his sock-encased hands and picked up some of the white powder, which he apparently found very tasty. Rocky gurgled, yelled and scooped up some more.

She laughed despite herself.

Splat!

A huge, sloppy snowball hit her right in the face.

He obviously knew nothing about snowballs. She wiped away the snow, picked up a handful and shaped it into a nice, hard round ball. She let fly. He tried to dodge but it caught him on the shoulder.

"Ouch," he yelled dramatically, grabbing his shoulder.

"That's for cheating at cards," she told him.

Quick as lightening, she shaped another and threw it. He did dodge that one, but leaned down and grabbed a handful of snow before he sought protection behind a tree.

She took shelter, scrunching down, doing her best to use tiny Rocky as a shield.

"Hey," he called. "Get away from that baby. That's not fair."

"All's fair in war," she called back. She left out the love part. How on earth could you love a man determined to be the world's biggest mystery? A man who cheated at cards? A man who had more passports than she had dresses?

She looked at Rocky.

And understood the world's biggest mystery was not in Ben, or in any man, but in love itself. It had found her. Sought her out in this isolated place where she had hidden from life, and from the mysteries of her own heart.

Somehow, someway, when she was not looking, and when she least expected it, she had fallen in love with this little waif who sat beside her in the snow, delighting in it. As for the big waif—

Splat. Right beside her. She scrambled to her feet and grabbed a huge handful of snow.

"What kind of man throws snowballs at a woman and child?" she demanded.

"A nasty one," he shot back.

If only she could believe that. If only she could hold fast to the belief that he was nasty, not worthy of her trust. And yet somehow a deeper part of her *knew*.

That he was a strong man.

He lived by a code of honor she might not understand but that was implacable all the same.

And that he was lonely in this life.

Almost as lonely as she was.

He shot out from behind the tree and ran for another one.

She could tell by the way he ran, crouched over, zigzagging, that he was trained in this kind of game. She knew that for him, it was not always a game.

Something in her heart lurched when she thought of that.

That he would leave here and go back into a world harsh and brutal. Where he would not be dodging snowballs.

She let the snowball fly, just as he zagged. It missed him.

He laughed heartily. She felt as if she was trying to save his laughter, to hold in her mind and in her heart. To take out on a different day, a small piece of him tucked inside her to keep. After he was gone.

She grabbed another handful of snow and let fly again. It hit the tree he ducked behind. Three snowballs in a row were tossed out from behind it, and they all hit her! With a cry of mock rage she stormed his fortress.

She ignored the snowballs zinging at her and ran toward him. He didn't run away, and she stuffed a great armload of snow down his shirt back, until he grabbed her wrists.

Suddenly the laughter died. His eyes fixed on her lips.

He let go so abruptly she nearly fell over. But not before she had seen the desire blaze through his eyes.

She stood there, stunned.

He wanted her.

"Help me build a snowman for him, before it melts."

Or maybe not. His tone was even, absolutely level, not at all like the tone of a man who had nearly lost control. Nearly kissed her. Nearly taken her in his arms and held her tight, so tight.

She was nearly breathless from thinking about it.

"Aren't you freezing?" she asked him, shocked to feel, deep inside her, just how ready she was to kindle a fire.

"Oh, sure, but I can get warm anytime, and this moment may never come again."

She thought of that. This moment may never come again.

And something wild rose within her. A woman, who wanted to know this man. Wanted him in every way it was possible for a woman to want.

After he left, she could get warm again.

But this moment might never come again.

"Come on," he said. "I remember a thing or two about snowmen from my Wyoming childhood."

Did she hear just a trace of sadness there, a yearning for something gone? Whatever he felt, it soon became apparent he had no ordinary snowman in mind. They pushed the first ball around her clearing, her shoulder right next to his. Brushing his. Their cold hands finding each other, clinging for a moment's warmth, pulling away.

She was finally grunting and groaning with exertion. The huge snowball they were now pushing left little trails of grass and mud behind it.

"It's big enough," she panted.

"Just about."

"Ben!"

"Maybe it's big enough for a kid who will get to see snowmen all the time, but it's not big enough for my baby. Not yet."

A funny gift for a baby, a beautiful gift for a baby.

He gave up when both of them, pushing as hard as they could, could barely budge the big ball. Rocky clapped excitedly when Ben brought him over to it.

The second ball was nearly as large as the first, which made it impossible to lift. It broke in half when they tried to lift it, and she found herself buried under a ton of wet stuff, spitting out snow and choking on laughter. Undaunted, Ben placed what was left of his half on top of the first ball, came and held out his hand to her, brushed her off.

She thought, *Now would be the time to kiss him.* She closed her eyes. She reached up on tiptoe. She nearly fell over, because he had turned away and was busy repairing the snowman, using rapidly melting snow for glue.

He made the head himself, sending her to search the clearing for the right rocks, large, dark and round to make eyes, sharp and pointy for the nose, small and square for the teeth.

Rocky crowed and clapped, and toppled over in his excitement. He started to cry when he felt the cold snow on his face.

Ben leaped forward to rescue him, picked him up and brushed the snow away. Though he was shivering now in his light shirt, he carried the baby all the way around the snowman several times, making adjustments, adding snow ears.

Storm went in and stoked the fire, put on some water and powdered milk to make hot chocolate.

Ben came in, finally, stamping his feet and talking to the baby.

She braced herself, waiting for him to *use* the laughter they had just shared to make a bid for the gun.

And when he didn't, she knew what was going to happen next.

She went out onto the porch and pried back the loose board. She reached down and found the gun. Holding it gingerly between her thumb and her index finger, she brought it in and laid it on the table before him.

He was sitting at the table, Rocky on his knee.

She folded her arms over her chest, watching, waiting.

He looked at her long and searchingly. Finally, he looked at the gun. He handed her the baby, and she watched as he carefully inspected it, then tucked it in the waistband of his jeans.

"Thanks," he said quietly. And they both knew it was for more than the gun. It was for something else.

A fragile thing in the air between them.

A thing neither of them had felt for so long. Too long.

Trust.

She shrugged and set the baby on the floor. Poured cocoa. She could feel him watching her.

"Why?" he finally said.

She wished he didn't have to have the words. She brought the cocoa to the table, and turned away to make one for Rocky, diluting it with water so it wouldn't be so hot. "I don't know."

"That's one," he said.

She laughed.

Then he said, "Yes, you do."

"All right. I do."

"And?"

She sighed. She took her hands and placed them on either side of his face. She gazed down at him.

"Because surely," she said, "I wouldn't want to do this so badly to someone I couldn't trust."

She kissed him.

His lips were wonderful. Her desire was so hot it melted her reason. She kissed him and felt some hard-held control break inside of him. And then he was kissing her back.

Hard and hungry.

He pulled her down onto his lap, and his hands ran over her curves until she was shivering with desire and wanting.

The storm had broken.

And as is often the way with storms, it felt good. A dam breaking, some finely held tension bursting. Drenching them both.

Wild, untamable.

Or at least she was unable to tame it.

He put her away, so suddenly she felt dazed trying to find her feet underneath her as he pushed her from his lap.

He stood up so swiftly the chair clattered over behind him.

"Storm, we can't. I can't."

She stared at him.

"You don't know what you're doing," he said softly. "You don't."

"Yes, I do!" She knew if she threw herself at him, he would not be able to refuse her a second time.

But she registered the stricken look on his face and suddenly didn't feel the things she had just felt—wild and womanly.

She felt rejected. Foolish.

"It's not that I don't want you," he said hoarsely. "It's not that. Storm, you are so beautiful. I want you more than the earth."

"Don't say anything else."

"But I can't have you. I'm not the kind of man you need."

"How can you know anything about what I need?"

"That's it precisely. We don't know the first thing about each other."

"Yes, we do."

"You need a man like one of your brothers. A nice, quiet, stable, strong man."

"You're the only man I ever met as strong as either of my brothers."

He ran a hand through his hair. "I have to go. I have to get out of here."

"Pardon?"

"I'm going to hike down to my radio today. I'll see what's developed."

"I thought you were going to do that in a week, which is in four more days."

"I can't wait." If he waited even another hour, he was pretty sure he'd do something he regretted. Take the trust that she had handed him when she gave him back his gun and prove himself unworthy.

Because you didn't make love with a woman like her once and walk away, as if she meant nothing. As if it was just an experience you were going to share that wasn't going to alter you both for all time.

There was only one way a man who hoped to retain his sanity was going to accept what she just offered.

He would have had to have given some serious consideration to what he wanted. Not just in the next hour or the next day or the next week, but what he wanted for a long, long time.

Forever.

Because Storm Taylor was a forever kind of girl. To think he could offer her any less would be to diminish her. But not as much as it would diminish him.

Hadn't he been thinking about what he was going to do with the rest of his life ever since he had taken that job with Noel?

What strange twist in his path had led him here?

Was he looking at the rest of his life when he looked into the bottomless blue of her eyes? How could that be? What had he ever done to deserve heaven?

He shook his head.

She was crying. Proudly. Silently. She wiped away a tear with an impatient hand.

"Shauna." Not Storm. But Shauna.

"Don't call me that."

"Shauna, I'm sorry."

"You know, men and women kiss each other every day. It's no big deal."

A meaner man might have said, *Well, then why are*

you crying? The man he had been last week might have said that.

Instead, he moved forward and gathered her in his arms and let her cry against his shoulder.

And when she was done, he put her away from him and said, "I'm going to go and check in with my radio now."

"You can't. You're soaked. Even your feet are wet."

He didn't say anything.

"You'll get hypothermia."

Again, he was silent.

She wouldn't look at him. "Are you taking the baby with you?"

"No."

They both knew that meant he was coming back. At least one more time.

Chapter Nine

Ben hiked down the mountain, trying manfully to ignore the fact she was right. His feet were already wet and cold from building the snowman. Slogging downhill through this slush was not helping matters. He decided the uncomfortable freezing sensation would be bearable if it was closer to his heart. It could put out the fire burning there.

A fire in your heart, he scoffed at himself. It wasn't even a physical possibility. A heart was a muscle that pumped blood. If he didn't watch himself, he'd be writing poetry soon. Eating granola. Meditating.

Come to think of it, Noel had practiced the art of meditation. Anywhere and anyplace. Long bus rides, busy train stations, the hard chairs of assembly halls. Ben would glance over and see that Noel's eyes were closed but that he was not sleeping. Thankfully, Noel's meditations did not involve any kind of embarrassing chanting or humming.

Though he had known Noel only a short time, Noel

had struck Ben as being one of the most peaceful and courageous individuals he had ever met. Calm and unflappable, even in the face of a hectic schedule, political chaos, the threats that came daily.

"Why do you do that?" Ben had asked Noel once, casually, of Noel's meditation.

"To remind me of what is real."

Ben thought a man shouldn't need reminding of that. Reach out and touch the nearest rock. Real. So why had he asked, "And what's that?"

Love is the only real thing. Everything else is illusion.

A good way to wind up dead, thinking like that.

He had briefed Storm, before he left, to be careful. To keep the shotgun loaded and her eyes and ears open. She hadn't really seemed to be listening.

No wonder. Kisses like that set hearts on fire. Turned off ears.

A good first line for a poem. Ha ha.

With any luck he would be back to her by nightfall. If you wanted to call that luck—being back in that little cabin with her for one more night. Her lips, her eyes, the swell of her breasts pushing against her shirt, the roundness of her behind—more like sweet torment than luck. No, luck would be if his and Rocky's need for sanctuary were over. If by tomorrow they could depart for places south.

Though his mind didn't want to go there, either.

What's going to happen to Rocky? she'd asked.

His baby. What was going to happen to his baby? Babies without families didn't do well in Crescada. Though his political advisers told Noel kids couldn't vote, Noel had used his newfound popularity with the press to point out terrible conditions in Crescada's orphanages. Ben could still see the rows of little cribs, babies needing changing, standing, smiling shyly, holding out their arms, begging mutely for attention.

He stopped walking and sank down on a rock. He felt worn right out. As vulnerable as he had ever felt.

Damn, he felt like he was going to cry.

"Hey, Noel," he shouted. "You up there?"

Noel had believed, with his whole heart and soul, that death was not an ending but a transition, spirit-changing energy, nothing more. He had not been afraid of it.

Silence.

"That's what I thought." Ben got up, brushed the wet snow from the seat of his pants. "If you were up there, I'd sure want to know what to do."

Be happy.

He did not know where the words came from. It seemed they came from inside of him, but those particular words were as foreign to his makeup as silver teapots, expensive champagne, designer clothes, Persian rugs.

"Oh, sure," he muttered, "it's that easy."

He did not know where this came from, either: a sudden mental image of him and Storm standing in the horse trough together, laughing. Him in that silly excuse for a bathtub singing his fool head off. Pushing that ridiculously large ball of snow around the clearing to make the world's biggest snowman for the baby.

Happiness. Could it be that simple? As simple as a man, a woman and a child being together? Laughing? Choosing love?

Love is the only real thing.

He acknowledged that he was not a philosophical

man. About the furthest thing from it, in fact. And yet he found a strangely philosophical thought crowding his mind. That what was *real* about Noel *had* survived. Noel's love had changed people around him. Changed the face of his nation.

Noel's love had not died when Noel had but lived on in the laughter of his child, the love that little boy would give the world.

But whose world was Rocky going to give his love to?

Ben had a bright and fleeting idea Storm might be able to adopt the baby, and then realized he was really going soft in the head. He might live out of a duffel bag, but she lived out of a saddle bag. She didn't know anything about babies, no more than he did.

Though he conceded both of them knew quite a lot more than they had just four short days ago. Maybe it wasn't that hard to learn.

Still, she'd be a single mom. He couldn't wish that burden on her, even though she was tough as nails.

That was only on the outside, anyway.

He knew that now. Inside she was soft. Beautiful. Tender.

Passionate.

Where the hell was that radio, anyway?

She probably wouldn't be alone for long if she had the baby. Some guy would have the good sense to marry her.

But what kind of guy? She was pretty innocent. She might pick a jerk. Her and Rocky with a jerk. All because he, Ben, didn't have the nerve to do what needed to be done.

And what is that? chided that very aggravating inner voice.

"Be happy!" he snapped back. "Where's the radio?" He put enough colorful adjectives between "the" and "radio" to make a longshoreman blush.

Which was another thing. He was not domesticated. Some men were. They knew what was required of them around the softer sex. They were sensitive, had good manners, didn't swear and had the decency to phone if they were going to be late. They noticed if their woman had gotten her hair cut, bought a new dress or changed the color of paint in the living room. Ben McKinnon did not have any of the characteristics of a Prince Charming, and he damned well knew it.

Though to give himself credit, he would certainly notice if Storm got her hair cut.

And the thought of her in *any* dress was enough to make his mouth go dry.

He thought of holding her in his arms while she cried just before he left and of the strange mixture of patience, protectiveness and tenderness he had felt.

"There's no way I could perform so perfectly on a daily basis," he muttered to himself. He took a compass reading and swore some more at the missing radio. He thought of being with her on a daily basis. Making her laugh. Watching the baby grow.

It occurred to him he wanted Rocky to have a pony. Play baseball. Make acorn owls with his kindergarten class. Eat ice cream on hot July afternoons.

He congratulated himself for managing to live most of his life without feeling. Because this sudden choking feeling he was experiencing only made everything more complicated. It made him feel confused, annoyed, angry, aggravated and—

Alive, that damned voice suggested impudently.

"Alive," he responded, "is a physical process, breathing in and out, nothing more."

Then he realized that was how he might have defined *alive* before he had come into the clearing of Heart's Rest. Now it was something else.

"Yeah, having a heart on fire." He scowled at his compass. "Which some people, myself included, would recognize as heartburn."

He realized he was talking to himself. Eleven years of doing the toughest, loneliest, hardest work known to man and he'd always managed to think his thoughts with quiet dignity. Four days in the company of a woman and a baby and he was babbling like an idiot. Talking to trees.

With a sigh of relief, he spotted the radio.

He didn't like using it. Radio transmissions were too easy to pinpoint with the right kind of equipment. That was why he had left this piece of expensive, very high-tech satellite equipment so far from the cabin.

He managed to rouse Jack. His heart fell further and further as he heard what Jack was saying. Crescada had fallen. Civil unrest had been ignited with Noel's death. Within three days the government had toppled. All except one of the people involved in Noel's assassination had been found and brought to justice.

"Where's the other one?" Ben asked.

"We're not sure."

"Is he after the baby?"

"*Your* baby?" Jack said with surprise.

Ben was sure he had said *the* baby. Must be a lousy transmission on both ends.

"There's no reason to believe he'd be after the

baby, Ben. It's over. What would the sense be of going after the baby now? They've lost."

But Ben knew what the bad guys did rarely made sense. If it did, it would make it so much easier for the good guys to always win. Some of these people were fanatical. An empire had toppled. People had used lesser reasons to seek revenge. People had vented their rage on innocents for far less reason than that.

"Ben, where can we meet you?"

Or was he trying to hang on to something that was gone? That was over and done with? Was he trying to think of a reason to stay at that cabin just a little while longer? To hold on to that little piece of heaven for a little while more?

That little piece of heaven, he reminded himself, that had him babbling to trees and feeling strange and powerful longings, the likes of which he had never felt before.

He'd trusted Jack's judgment for the past eleven years. They had placed their lives in each other's hands on many occasions. If Jack said it was safe to come out, it was.

"Prince George," he said. "I'll be at the airport in Prince George late tomorrow afternoon."

He terminated the connection. The world suddenly seemed very silent. Empty.

And then a familiar sound crept into the emptiness. So distant, at first he had to strain his ears to make sure he was hearing properly. But he knew that sound and he would know it anywhere. It grew louder.

It was definitely the steady beat of chopper blades. A helicopter.

He had never felt anything like the fear he felt as

he raced, crashing through bushes, having branches whip his face and arms, back toward the cabin. And his baby. And his woman.

The door of the cabin whispered open.

Storm looked over at the big man who filled the doorway, disappointed it wasn't Ben.

"Hello, big brother."

"What the hell?" Jake said, staring at the baby who was playing quietly on the sleeping bag with his teddy bear.

Storm looked over her shoulder. It had been a perfect day to get the dishes dusted out and ready for the clients. She had a sink full of hot soapy water. "Did Stanley drop you off? I saw the forestry chopper."

"Yeah." Jake stared hard at the little person on the sleeping bag. Finally, he appeared to gather his wits. "Is that a baby?"

"No, it's a puppy."

Jake gave her a dark look.

"Okay. It is. A baby. Where did Stanley drop you off? Did you have to walk far?"

"Naw. A couple of miles. A baby?"

"Jake," she said gently, "we've established it's a baby."

"Okay. How about if we establish whose baby? You don't have clients booked for a few weeks yet."

"Well, if it was mine, even you would have noticed something over the last nine months. I think."

He was looking at her with such horror that she realized her brother actually was considering the possibility she had come up here to secretly have a baby. She knew it would only confuse things further if she pointed out to him that this was obviously no new-born on her sleeping bag.

"The baby is not mine, Jake. Sit down. I'll make some cocoa and tell you the whole story. Do you want to hold him?"

"God, no!" Jake took a seat and eyed the baby warily, as if he expected Rocky to scoot across the floor and bite his ankle.

Storm ignored his no, scooped up Rocky and put him on her brother's lap. Jake glared at her. Big men looked good with small babies. Strangely, it was her brother who looked helpless and not the baby, who was staring at Jake with avid interest.

Rocky tried out one of his award-winning smiles on her brother. Jake glanced at her, then smiled back, a little bit cautiously.

Storm thought her brother was really quite a good-looking man when he smiled. Which was not that often.

Too much responsibility too young.

Because of her. She'd only been a few years older than this baby when her parents had died, and Jake, just seventeen, had taken it all on.

She went back to the sink and filled the big black iron kettle she used on the wood stove. She glanced back. The baby had a hold of Jake's index finger and was trying to cram it in his mouth.

Jake laughed. "He's a kind of cute little feller, isn't he?"

"I think so."

She came and sat at the table.

Her brother looked at her, and suddenly she knew he saw far more than she thought he did, because the laughter died abruptly in his eyes. "Storm, what's the matter?"

"Nothing." Her mouth trembled when she said it.

"You better tell me what's going on."

She tried to smile. "What are you doing here?"

"I had some time free up. I thought I'd come up and give you a hand with the chain saw. But never mind that, little girl, tell me what's going on up here."

"I'm not a little girl anymore, Jake. I'm a woman." And with that she burst into tears. Her brother awkwardly juggled the baby so that he could slam her on the back with his free hand, a gesture she was pretty sure he intended to be comforting.

Drying her eyes on her sleeve, she told him. About Ben showing up in the clearing with the baby. About the gun. And the passports. And the truth, or what she hoped was the truth.

"Did he hurt you?" Jake asked, his tone low, lethal and killing.

"Of course not!"

"Then why are you bawling like that?"

"Oh, Jake, I'm so mixed up."

Understanding dawned in Jake's face. "I'm going to kill him," he decided.

"Jake, you don't understand."

"Yes, I do. I know what men are like. The snake."

"Jake, nothing happened!"

Jake did not look convinced.

The door burst open behind them.

"Put the baby down, then your hands where I can see them. And turn around slowly. Don't try anything."

"Ben!"

She almost did not recognize him, the look on his face was so cold, so intense. Jake handed her Rocky and pushed back from the chair, slowly, his hands in the air.

He turned.

Ben looked confused, obviously seeing in Jake's face, and in Storm's, that the situation was not what he thought it was.

"Ben, this is my brother Jake."

He dropped the gun to his side and stared, then ran a hand through his hair. "Jake. Jeez. I'm sorry." He moved forward, his hand out.

Jake charged him like a bull. Ben didn't have time to react. Jake's shoulder hit him in the stomach and they both tumbled out the door.

"Stop it!" Storm ordered. She flew out the door after them. They had tumbled down the steps. The gun, thankfully, was on the landing.

Jake had straddled Ben's chest and was pounding his face with his big fists.

In a move so fast, Storm didn't even know what had happened, Ben used his legs and somehow tossed Jake over his head. In a flash their positions were reversed, and Ben had straddled her brother. Which wasn't stopping her brother from punching Ben with all his considerable might.

"Stop it," she cried.

She might as well have gone in the cabin and shut the door.

She picked up the gun. She studied it for a moment, checked the chamber, found the safety. She took it off.

She aimed it at the sky and pulled the trigger.

Boom!

They froze.

"You guys stop it right now."

Ben, his fist still raised, looked over his shoulder at her. Jake stopped pummeling the man on top of him. Slowly, Ben stepped off her brother. He hesitated and then held out his hand to him.

Jake hesitated and then took the extended hand. Ben heaved him up.

They stood there regarding each other for a wary moment.

"Jeez," Ben said. "You fight as well as your sister arm wrestles. What do they put in the water up here?"

Jake regarded him for a minute and then grinned sheepishly. He had blood coming off the corner of his mouth. He held out his hand.

Ben took it, and they shook. Then they were both coming toward her.

Ben was bleeding from his nose.

"Is that broken?" she asked him.

Jake studied Ben's nose, reached out and gave it a little shove with his finger. "I think it might be, Storm."

"Not the first time," Ben said.

"Me, either," Jake said. "Busted mine the first time when I was fourteen. Riding a steer in the back lot."

"Hey, that's how I broke mine the first time!" Ben said.

The two men brushed by her and went into the cabin.

"On a steer?" Jake said. "You from a farm family?"

"Ranch. Wyoming. We raised Herefords. My old man dabbled in quarter horses on the side."

"Really?"

Storm stood and watched them with her hands on her hips. They were going to be friends now?

She stomped by them and got them each a damp cloth.

Jake held his to his mouth, Ben dabbed at his nose, spreading blood all over until she couldn't stand it. She went and took the cloth from him and did it for him.

She was aware of a sudden silence, of Jake and Ben both watching her with fascination.

"What?" Storm asked.

Jake looked at Ben. "My sister has feelings for you."

"Jake!"

"And if you took advantage of her, I'm going to kill you." This was announced flatly, matter-of-factly.

"Jake!"

"If I'd taken advantage of your sister, that's what I'd deserve," Ben responded quietly.

Her brother regarded Ben thoughtfully, then grinned, and they started talking about cattle again! Artificial insemination versus keeping a bull.

She glared at the pair of them. "I do not have feelings for him," she informed her brother, in a hiss as she banged a hot chocolate down in front of him.

He looked at the spot on his shirt where some of it splashed. "Well, all right," he said dubiously. "There's no need to start throwing the hot chocolate around."

Ben was looking at his cup, stirring the chocolate over and over. He glanced up at her brother, he looked at the baby, he looked everywhere. Except at her.

That's when she knew he was leaving.

"Did you raise someone on the radio?" she asked, her voice controlled, almost uncaring.

His eyes, finally, came to rest on her face. And she knew she had not convinced him any more than she had convinced her brother.

"Yes."

"And?"

"I have to go."

Her eyes smarted, like she'd been peeling onions.

"Rocky and I have to go," he amended.

"When?" It came out wrong. Like a little squeak of dismay.

Jake was looking hard at her now, but scared enough of wearing that hot chocolate that he didn't say anything.

"I have to be in Prince George tomorrow."

"How are you going to get there?" Jake asked, always the practical one. "You got a car hidden somewhere?"

"Not exactly. Not where I can get at it."

"Where is it?" Jake asked.

"The bottom of the river. Storm told you everything, right?"

"I guess. Most everything. What kind of car was it?"

"Some sort of sedan. New. Rent-a-car."

"You have to pay for that?" Jake asked.

"Who cares?" Storm snapped.

Jake looked at her with slow hurt. "Was just asking."

"It's okay," Ben said. "Yeah, we'll have to pay for it."

Jake actually chuckled, as if he was enjoying this

conversation. "I bet the boss will have a few words to say to you about that."

Ben smiled. "You've got that right."

It occurred to Storm these two men would make fast friends if they got to know each other. Which they weren't going to do.

"Jake, you guys can take the horses down to my truck. Ben and the baby can stay at the ranch overnight and you can drive them to Prince George in the morning. I've got plenty to do up here that doesn't require a horse."

She thought she'd said that crisply, emotionlessly, but Jake seemed to hear the sadness in her voice.

"Yes, ma'am," he said. He didn't even make her arm wrestle about it. "I'll bring the horses back for you in a day or two."

"Whatever," she said, not able to trust herself to say more.

Jake nodded. Ben wouldn't look at her.

Suddenly all that work outside, all the trees that needed to be cleared, didn't even seem to compare to what needed doing inside.

She needed to do a housecleaning on her heart.

Pick up all those broken pieces that had sat in there too long.

Of course, suddenly she recognized that wasn't true. Dorian had not broken her heart. He had only made her afraid to trust herself.

And really, when she looked at that, it was not her instincts that let her down. It was the fact she had not listened to them.

Overridden them at every possible turn. Ignored what they had whispered, then shouted and then screamed.

"Excuse me," she said.

"Where you going?" Jake asked.

She shrugged. She wasn't going anywhere, except away from them. She had to be by herself, to listen to herself. It was hard to do that with Ben in a room. He seemed to clutter up her thinking process.

Make her think wild thoughts. Of being kissed by him. Held by him. Loved by him.

He made her think funny thoughts of babies and cottages with little curtains.

Forever.

Had there ever been a man less likely to promise anyone forever than Ben McKinnon?

"We'll have to push off pretty soon, Storm," her brother said.

"Well then," she said with forced brightness. "I'll just say my goodbyes now. Goodbye, Ben." She looked somewhere over his left shoulder instead of right at him. She thought of offering him her hand but knew she could not.

Storm looked at the baby, and the words would not come past the lump in her throat.

She stumbled over to Rocky, picked him up and cradled him against her. She breathed deeply his baby scent, touched his hair and smoothed it down, trying to memorize the feel of that silky tuft under her fingers.

She held him back from her and gazed at his round cheeks, the bright intelligence of his dark eyes. She looked at his long lashes, at the little pout of his mouth and the shape of his ears.

"Orm," he crowed. "Orm-orm."

Silly to think he might be trying to call her name. It could only make everything worse if she believed that Baby had become as attached to her as she had become to him.

In a moment, she would embarrass herself.

She would beg Ben to let her have the baby. To keep him forever safe with her. To let her give him what he needed most.

Not that she really was any kind of expert on what babies needed.

But she did know what this baby needed most.

Love.

That simply.

But she couldn't just keep a baby because she loved him. If it was that easy, Ben would keep this baby.

Because she could see him looking now, at Rocky, and his love for that baby was naked in his handsome face.

It was that look that she wanted to remember. Ben's rugged face taut with tenderness, with longing, with regret.

She set the baby down on the sleeping bag. Fighting down the terrible clawing at her throat, she ran out the door.

She ran across the clearing and into her woods. As soon as the shadows embraced and hid her, she collapsed into the damp and fragrant needles that carpeted the forest floor.

She put her head on her arms and finally, there, she cried.

Chapter Ten

Ben watched the look on her brother's face as Storm ran out the door. He wasn't sure he was going to get out of here alive, yet. Jake was taller than him by a full inch and probably outweighed him by thirty pounds.

That scuffle in the yard was about as much of a tangle as he wanted with this big man.

But Jake only looked at him sadly and said, "I don't think I'll ever understand women. And Storm's a lot easier to understand than most of them."

Ben said nothing.

"Do you have feelings for her?" Jake asked.

Ben took a deep breath. "Have feelings for her?" he echoed. Wasn't it obvious that he was one giant feeling right now? That the man who sat here calmly sipping cocoa was only a cardboard cutout, a facade? That the real man behind that cutout wanted, desperately, to get up and run after her?

Make everything all right between them.

Thank her, at least, for sharing her refuge with him for a few days.

Jake was looking at him expectantly.

"Maybe we should pack up that baby and go," Ben suggested, with a cool, steely edge to his voice that he recognized.

Jake didn't let him off that easy. He studied him long and hard before he finally nodded slowly and said, "You strike me as the kind of man who will do the right thing."

Ben sensed it was high praise and was not at all sure that he deserved it. Because what did that mean, the right thing? The right thing for whom? For Storm? For the baby? For himself?

Was it possible the right thing could be the same thing for all three of them?

No. The right thing felt like it would be to walk away from all this. Reclaim his old life. By next week he could be on assignment somewhere else, using his wits and his experience to be among the best in his line of work, to survive. Why did the prospect suddenly seem exhausting?

Maybe because it really wasn't the right thing. Maybe it was only the comfortable thing, the easy thing. The familiarity of it beckoned, promised him order and control.

Maybe, sometimes, the right thing was to go out on a limb, to do something differently than he had ever done it before. Or listen to the yearnings of his own heart. To understand the emptiness within him was meant to be filled.

Jake came and patted him on the shoulder, a gesture Ben thought was probably meant to be reassuring, though the man's hands were so big, and Jake was so strong, it felt more like that bashing on his back was rattling his teeth.

"It'll all work out," Jake said.

Side by side, they packed up the baby's things and then went out and got the horses ready to go. Ben acknowledged how good it felt to be around horses. Suddenly, he wished for simplicity in his life: horses, cattle and hard work.

Of course, simplicity would not include a woman and a baby.

They had only one saddle, but Jake had no problem riding bareback. He handed the baby up to Ben, who placed him in the saddle in front of him.

Some of his own earliest memories were of this: sitting in the saddle in front of his father. He wrapped one arm securely around the baby, took up the reins with the other.

"I'll bring the horses back for her tomorrow," Jake said, "and give her a hand clearing those trails. It's too big a job for a woman, 'specially a small one like her, not that she could ever admit that."

"Yeah," Ben said. "She's not good at admitting when she's not good at something." As if he was now some kind of expert on her.

He didn't want to think of her up here alone. Hiding from herself. Her passion. He just wanted to ride away, like the cowboy in the movies, with never a glance back. Not that the cowboy in the movies was ever sharing his saddle with a baby. Despite his resolve not to, Ben looked back.

And his gaze came to her sign, black letters singed into wood: Heart's Rest.

He felt an odd burning behind his eyes. It was as if all the world was suddenly illuminated, as if he had never before been able to see and now he could. The red on the Indian paintbrush was brilliant, the green of her grass deep and true, the cottage itself postcard pretty, the red checked curtains showing from the outside, the empty rocking chair on the porch. He turned swiftly to face forward.

He chased the regret away with an emotion he understood better. Anger.

It was a damn good thing he was leaving. Another few days and who knows what he would have become? His world felt all topsy-turvy and uncertain, and he didn't like that one bit.

He was going back to his old life. Of course he was! Had he ever really contemplated giving up his life of danger and excitement? So what if it was occasionally mixed with tedium and loneliness?

But what about seeing people die? Hadn't he had his fill of that, even before Noel? He'd done his share to make the world a better place. Quite frankly, he did not feel he had succeeded. Maybe it was a job that needed to be left, now, to younger men. Those fresh-faced young guys who came through the FIA training facility so full of idealism.

But what did he think he was going to do? Set up housekeeping in the deep woods with her? What would he do all day? Make a relationship the biggest compartment in his life? Ha!

"The ranch next door to ours is for sale," Jake said, apparently with no ulterior motive, just making conversation.

"Is that right?" Ben said, flatly, just making conversation.

"Nice place. The old couple who run it are retiring. The Petersens. Their kids aren't interested. It's hard country. You have to be tougher than old boot leather to make it at ranching in this part of the world.''

Was there a bit of a challenge in that? Ben glared at the broad back in front of him.

"All the cattle and machinery and everything will go with it.''

"That's real nice,'' Ben said. He could hear the hardness in his own voice, again, and it felt familiar and good.

Jake sent him a look over his shoulder, and then thankfully was quiet for the rest of the long ride down Storm's Mountain.

The baby tried chewing the saddle horn and the horse's mane. He talked to himself, happy gibberish. Then he yelled "Beb-beb" and pointed so wildly at a squirrel racing up a tree that he nearly threw himself off the horse. Ben wrapped his arm around Rocky a little more securely, felt all the energy in that squirming little bundle of life.

"Squirrel,'' he told the baby and thought, such a simple thing, a life. And yet not simple at all.

And that's when Ben faced the truth. He had let love in.

And his heart was never going to be totally hard again no matter what he did; no matter how powerfully he tried to get back to who he had been a week ago, he could not. That man was gone, and a new one had taken his place.

"That's what you think,'' he said sternly.

Jake turned and gave him an odd look. "Did you say something?''

"No.''

His heart was never going to be the same again? It would be nice if he could stop talking to himself!

They rode off the mountain. At the bottom of the trail was another corral and an old truck. Jake had trouble starting it. Ben noticed the rabbit's foot hanging from the mirror and dug through Rocky's pack for a tiny pair of Adidas shoes. He knotted the laces together and draped them over the mirror.

Jake raised an eyebrow at him.

"She won them in a poker game, fair and square," he lied, one of those necessary lies. The truth was he wanted her to have something to remember them by. Him and the baby.

The country her brother had described as hard seemed to him to be indescribably beautiful, rolling foothills, good grass, pole fences, fat cattle, the mountains in the near distance.

After a long drive over bad roads, they crossed under a signpost that said they were on the Taylor Ranch. It looked as if the family had been here since the beginning of time. The log barns were old and weathered gray. Their house was a simple, white-clapboard two-storey. Pulling up in front of it, Ben saw red checkered curtains at one of the windows.

He got out of the truck and the first thing he saw was the flower beds lining the front walk. He told himself he had seen hundreds of flower beds in his life. There was really no reason for the lump in his throat, no reason to see her crouched there with dirt on her hands, and probably on her nose, bringing something of herself to this wild place. Bringing something feminine to a place predominantly masculine.

Inside the house was the same—a predominantly masculine house, that honored function rather than esthetics, and yet her small touches were everywhere, and everywhere that they were danced with color and life. Here was a striped saddle blanket mounted on the living room wall, there was a dried-flower arrangement in a hand-thrown pot. It spoke to him not of Storm but of Shauna.

Her other brother, Evan, came in, very like her in looks—dark hair, that astonishing color in his eyes. In nature, he could have been a carbon copy of Jake, a man of few words.

After introductions were made, they found a playpen in the basement.

"This used to be Storm's," Evan told him, his affection for his sister raw in his voice.

"We'll put you in her room tonight."

"The couch is fine," Ben protested.

"Why would you sleep on the couch when we have a perfectly good bed?" Evan asked.

How could he say he did not want to sleep in her bed? Her room? That he did not want to know the things her room would tell him about her?

The brothers fed him the kind of meal he remembered from a long time ago. Thick steaks—barbecued—baked potatoes, salad.

He helped them feed cattle that night, liked working beside them in comfortable silence, liked the way the work made his muscles coil and jump, made him feel alive in a way he had not for a long, long time.

Then he was in her room, with the baby and the playpen. He set it up and put Rocky in it. The baby went to sleep instantly. He wanted to do the same. To not even look. But he could not.

There were several framed pictures of her in various stages of growing up. A pretty little girl with pigtails and a gap-toothed smile. In one she had a baby raccoon on her shoulder, in another she had her arms around a colt that looked unbelievably like his Jasper from long ago.

There was a weaving on one wall, brushes neatly lined up on her dresser.

He went over to her dresser. Snapshots of her brothers were tucked into the mirror claws. No picture of the boyfriend that she *should* have had. Why was he so glad she didn't have one? What on earth did that have to do with him?

He told himself not to open the drawer. Ordered himself not to.

But he did anyway. And looked at a little square of material that he didn't understand until he took it out.

A miniskirt. His mouth went dry. He put the skirt back and swiftly shut the drawer, forced himself to take off his own shirt and pants and climb in between sheets that smelled faintly, deliciously of her.

He told himself it was the little noises the baby made that kept him awake. Not the smell of her on the pillowcase. Not the walls of her room, plain and unpretentious just like her.

There was nothing frilly in her room. Not a jewel box or an earring case. No little doodads, crystal perfume containers, not even a stuffed dog.

Was that because she really didn't care about those things? Or because she tried not to care about those things? Would he ever know now? It seemed imperative that he know. He tossed and turned all night, mulling over all the things he did not know and would never know now.

The next day, he found clean clothes at the end of his bed. He showered in hot water. How could anybody yearn for that primitive and uncomfortable galvanized tub? Then the brothers fed him an enormous breakfast.

They wouldn't leave until they dug Storm's old baby car seat out of one of the sheds. And then Evan drove him to Prince George. It was a long drive. It reminded him of the immensity of this country.

In such an immense country, how had he found her? Unless there were such things as miracles?

Jack was waiting inside the airport. A woman was with him. Jack introduced Ms. Jenkins as a nurse with a degree in social work. She looked like a matronly type, old and stern.

"She's going to accompany the baby back to Crescada," Jack said. "And we need to get you back to headquarters for a debriefing."

The woman reached for the baby.

Ben's grip tightened on Rocky and he turned his shoulder into her.

Her arms dropped, and she took a step back, looking at Jack for guidance.

"The boss said you'd have to have some trauma counseling, because of Noel. Dr. Pickleblain has set something up."

That aggravating woman reached for the baby again.

"I'm taking him back to Crescada," Ben announced.

"Pardon?" Jack said.

"I'm taking Rocky back."

"Ben, that's not necessary. Ms. Jenkins here is supremely qualified, aren't you, Ms. Jenkins?"

Ms. Jenkins rattled off her degrees. Very impressive, but far more than a small baby needed. A small baby just needed someone to love him. Someone to correctly interpret "Beb-beb." Someone who could do a reasonable imitation of a choo-choo train when it came to peas and other inedible things.

Ms. Jenkins was definitely not a choo-choo train type. She looked as if she would think peas were edible. Ben was trained to read people, and he knew that for sure.

Besides, she didn't look at the baby in the right way. There was no underlying affection in her eyes when she looked at him, the way there always had been in Storm's. Ms. Jenkins looked professional and disinterested. Detached. She would just follow orders, whatever they were. She might not even check to make sure they were in the best interests of the baby.

"What arrangements have been made for him in Crescada?" Ben asked.

"I don't know, Ben. Who cares? Ms. Jenkins will look after it."

Who cares? Ben looked at his friend and wondered what this job did to men over years. What kind of person could say "who cares" about a little baby? As if he was nothing?

"I care," he heard himself say.

"You know, Ben," Jack said, gently, "that's a dangerous thing to do in this business."

Ben glared at Ms. Jenkins who looked as if she was going to make another attempt to take the baby from him.

"You know, Jack," Ben said, gently, "the most dangerous thing of all is to go through this life not caring."

Jack looked at him. "Where the hell have you been, anyway? Over the rainbow?"

Ben was looking at the ceiling-mounted incoming-flight monitor, wondering about the fastest route to Crescada. "Can I have her plane ticket?" he asked, nodding at Ms. Jenkins.

He knew what he was going to do. Go to Crescada and find the baby a good home. Not an orphanage. He had met some truly wonderful people through Noel. He would find somebody whose face just lit up when he passed that baby to them.

Like Storm's had lit up.

He went to the nearest ticket agent, and after some wrangling they had made arrangements about the tickets.

"I need some money," he told Jack. "I lost my last twenty in a poker game."

"I thought you were going to an empty cabin," Jack said, casting him a look, before reaching for his wallet.

"The universe had another plan for me."

"The universe?" Jack looked shocked.

What else could it be but a universal plan? When a man determined not to love was brought love anyway, in spite of himself? Was brought love in the middle of a country so immense it was beyond imagining? Was brought to a woman who needed him? And it was the very woman he also needed? What else could it be when a man who thought he lived a full life and a useful life was suddenly shown he was living in one dimension instead of three, in black and white instead of color?

He did not think he had done one thing in his life to make him worthy of the love he had found. With this baby.

With her.

"What the hell happened to you up there?" Jack asked.

"I think," Ben said slowly, articulating it out loud for the first time, "I think I found heaven."

They called his flight. He put the baby's bag over his shoulder, tucked Rocky under his arm like a little football and headed for the gate.

Storm watched the sun sinking over the peak of the mountain. In the corral behind her, she could hear Sam softly wuffling.

Ten days had passed since she had stood, concealed, at the edge of the clearing, watching Ben and Rocky ride away. She had not shown herself, had not been able to trust herself to say goodbye without crying, without begging to hold the baby one last time.

Watching them leave her clearing, she had felt panicky. Had Ben remembered Rocky's teddy bear? But she had controlled the panic, knowing it was really about something else. She had watched as Ben glanced back, his gaze resting on her sign for a moment, something in that look so naked that she had suddenly known something that she was not sure he knew himself.

He would come back this way. She did not know when or how but she knew his heart would draw him back to this place one day.

That night and the next day, she had waited for the sadness to come again, to cry more tears, but those things had not happened. She had thought the emptiness left by him and by the baby would make her feel small and so alone in the world.

Instead she felt oddly rich. As if her world had been made fuller than she could have ever imagined. She recognized she was changed in some fundamental way for loving those two males. One so very small. And one so very big.

She found she did not feel afraid of love anymore.

Or afraid of herself, the way she had felt after Dorian.

Storm recognized something now. That inner voice that had guided her down the pathways of her life had not abandoned her in Edmonton.

She had abandoned it. There had been so much noise and activity. University papers due, cars roaring by, telephones ringing, new information to sort through—so much happening all the time that she had forgotten how to be still.

How to listen to the voice inside her.

Now that she thought about it, it had tried to tell her the truth about Dorian. But she had not listened. On their first date, he had been rude to the doorman at the theater, and she had brushed aside the jolt of discomfort she felt. The next time he had lied to a waitress, saying it was his birthday in order to get a free drink, and she had laughed along with him, though her soul had shrunk from this deception. She had told herself she just didn't know how sophisticated people behaved. He had been evasive about his family, his work, the reasons he didn't call regularly, and she had made as many excuses for him as he had made for himself.

Because she had been young and naive and so fresh off the mountain. Because she had thought the gift the mountain gave her—her intuition—belonged only on the mountain and would have no place among the bustle of the city, sophisticated people and their ways.

Ben had lied to her, too, she told herself.

And then she smiled. Because Ben's lies had not been about him but about *them*. About his doing everything in his power to protect that baby and, ultimately, her.

Maybe in this world there were good lies and bad lies, after all.

So she asked it, the voice within her, the truth about Ben; she liked the answer it gave her.

That he was the other half of her soul.

And that nothing could change that. Not thousands of miles, not seconds ticking by on a clock, not days going by on a calendar.

And when she asked her inner voice about the baby, if the child she had come to cherish would be all right, her answer also came. Ben might not have said the words, he might not have even admitted it to himself, but he loved that baby. She could trust he would do the right thing for Rocky. Ben would not leave him, would not rest until he had made sure Rocky would have safety, happiness and love.

She had been down off the mountain, briefly, a week ago, to visit her brothers, to pick up supplies, to make last-minute phone calls to clients coming next week. Her truck had a pair of tiny running shoes hanging off the mirror. She had touched them as if they were a promise.

The ranch next door to her childhood home, the Petersen spread, had a big red Sold sticker over the For Sale sign that hung at the end of their long drive.

She had always thought she would buy that ranch. But she didn't really feel sad about that either. A universe that could conspire to bring her soul mate around the world to her could really do anything at all.

A twig snapped.

She was being watched, she knew it.

She continued to rock the chair, gently, almost lazily, pushing against the weathered grain of the porch floor with one foot. She wasn't worried. Not yet. The old pump-action shotgun resting outside the cabin's door, an arm's length away, gave her a sense of security.

It was probably an animal.

She was accustomed to that sensation, of thinking she was alone, in the bush, a million miles from the nearest human being, when suddenly she would feel it. Watched. Sometimes she would catch a glimpse of the woodland spy—the flick of a deer's tail, the back end of a bear going the other way—but usually she did not.

Everything was normal. But the sensation of being watched did not go away. She knew intuitively it was not an animal out there watching.

In fact, she knew, intuitively, exactly who it was. Her heart began to hammer an erratic rhythm within her breast.

"Might as well come out," she called, "I know you're there."

Silence.

She stretched out, reached her shotgun, casually pumped a round into the chamber.

Boom!

A horse came charging out of the trees.

A horse and a rider.

Ben McKinnon looked as if he was born to ride a horse.

"You spooked my horse, Storm."

She grinned, and her grin widened when over his

shoulder she caught sight of Rocky, staring at her with his black button eyes, one hand wrapped vigorously in Ben's hair.

Rocky's smile of recognition put her pretty close to heaven.

"That's not your horse," she said. "I'd recognize him anywhere. That's old Slewfoot. Belongs to the Petersen ranch next door to Jake and Evan and me."

"Slewfoot is no kind of name for a noble beast such as this. You people in this country need to learn about naming your animals."

"And you've returned to teach us?" Bantering with him felt so right, so like coming home.

"Well, for an example, I would call this horse—" he regarded his mount solemnly for a moment "—Jasper the Second."

"That's quite a handle for a swaybacked nag."

"Swaybacked nag? Take it back."

"And if I don't?"

"The next time it snows, you'll be sorry."

"I'm not expecting snow until November."

"I can wait."

Her heart beat even faster at those words. She watched as he dismounted from the horse, careful of the baby on his back. She stood up and came down the stone steps of her cabin, slowly, as if in a dream.

Slowly, until she saw the look in his eyes when he turned toward her.

She began to run.

And then she was in his arms and he was swinging her around, shouting to the tops of the mountains. Hugging her close to him, kissing her all over.

If Rocky's smile had put her close, this opened the door and let her in.

To heaven.

Rocky regarded all this solemnly over Ben's big shoulder.

"Ben, you still have him. You still have Rocky." She went around behind him and loosened the straps that secured the baby. At least he was in a proper holder this time.

She pulled Rocky into her arms and buried her nose in his neck, thinking she would never get enough of his sweet smell.

She began to cry. Tears of joy, that life could be so good.

And then Ben was there, gathering them both into his arms.

They stood like that for a long time, in their circle of love, but soon even their warmth could not keep the chill of the evening from them. They put the horse away, and then they moved inside.

They sat at the table, the baby drowsing against her shoulder.

"I went to bring him back," Ben said. "But I knew what orphanages in Crescada were like. I couldn't leave my baby there. I couldn't. So I started looking up friends and political acquaintances of Noel's thinking I would kind of interview them to find the one who could love the baby best of all.

"It took me a week to discover that no one could love this baby better than me. So I went to see about adopting him. The agency helped me cut through some of the red tape. And in a few weeks, it will be official."

"He'll be yours?"

"Not exactly, Storm."

"Not exactly?"

"He'll be ours."

"Ben, if I'm going to have a baby, my brothers are going to demand a wedding, by shotgun if necessary."

"You people in this country need some instruction on the proper use of shotguns."

"And you've returned to teach us?"

"I figure it's probably going to be a lifetime job. Teaching you."

"Hmm. Let's get started."

"Where would you suggest, ma'am?"

She touched her lips with her fingertips. "How about right here?"

"Really, Storm, in front of the children?"

"He's nearly sleeping!"

"I haven't even made it official yet."

"What? Kissing 101? You need a certificate for that?"

"I need to know you're going to marry me before I kiss the bride-to-be."

"Of course, I'm going to marry you. I already told you. By shotgun if necessary."

"It's not necessary. But this is. A declaration of love. An old-fashioned proposal. An engagement gift."

"Let's just kiss," she muttered.

"Storm, for shame. You should know something about me before we even discuss weightier issues."

"I know everything about you," she said.

"Really? That's quite a statement based on the strength of our lengthy, four-day relationship."

"Well, it's true. I know what's in your eyes when you look at Rocky. And at me. I know what's in your soul. What else is there to know?"

"I'm not with the agency anymore, Storm."

"And you're not sorry, right?"

"Actually, I'm not. I'm relieved."

"Okay, so we've talked about that now. Anything else?" She closed her eyes and leaned toward him.

"You want kisses before you know what I'm going to do for a living?"

"Ben, I don't care about the little things."

"That's a little thing?"

She kissed him then. "What do you think?"

"That all the world pales in comparison to that," he muttered.

"Exactly," she said, nibbling his ear.

"Just one more little thing? Please?"

"Make it quick, buster."

He reached into his breast pocket and pulled out a creamy piece of parchment. "Here's a little thing for you."

It was the deed to the Petersen ranch.

"Oh, Ben!"

"That's what I want to do. That's what I grew up doing. A part of me never left the ranch. It's as if I left my heart there. Or at least that's what I thought at first. Then when I was back in Crescada, I thought I had left it here at Heart's Rest. And I found out that wasn't quite true, either."

"And what's true, Ben? In forty words or less?"

"It was you. You are my heart's rest."

"Okay," she said, "is that it? The proposal, the gift, the declaration of love?"

"I guess it is." He gazed around, at her, at his baby. "You know life could really not get much more fair than this."

"Oh, I think it's got a good surprise or two left,"

she said, and then, her voice suddenly husky, and very serious she added, "You are my heart's rest, also. I'll go put the baby on the bag. He's sleeping now. And then, Ben?"

"Yes, sweetheart?"

"We need to get started on these kissing lessons. We've only got a lifetime."

He watched her put the baby down, kiss him on his round cheek, turn and come back across the cabin toward him, her love and her joy shining in her eyes.

And then he realized life really could get more fair than this. Better and more beautiful every single day. Full, as she had promised, of the most delightful surprises.

The taste of her lips. The light in her eyes. The way she would look when she was pregnant.

He opened his arms and she came into them, softly. And his heart, suddenly so much more than just an organ that pumped blood, found what it had always searched for.

Rest. Peace. The only thing that was real.

Love.

*   *   *   *   *

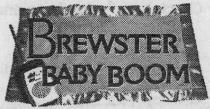
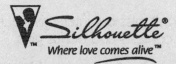

SILHOUETTE'S 20ᵀᴴ ANNIVERSARY CONTEST
OFFICIAL RULES
NO PURCHASE NECESSARY TO ENTER

1. To enter, follow directions published in the offer to which you are responding. Contest begins 1/1/00 and ends on 8/24/00 (the "Promotion Period"). Method of entry may vary. Mailed entries must be postmarked by 8/24/00, and received by 8/31/00.

2. During the Promotion Period, the Contest may be presented via the Internet. Entry via the Internet may be restricted to residents of certain geographic areas that are disclosed on the Web site. To enter via the Internet, if you are a resident of a geographic area in which Internet entry is permissible, follow the directions displayed on-line, including typing your essay of 100 words or fewer telling us "Where In The World Your Love Will Come Alive." On-line entries must be received by 11:59 p.m. Eastern Standard time on 8/24/00. Limit one e-mail entry per person, household and e-mail address per day, per presentation. If you are a resident of a geographic area in which entry via the Internet is permissible, you may, in lieu of submitting an entry on-line, enter by mail, by hand-printing your name, address, telephone number and contest number/name on an 8"x 11" plain piece of paper and telling us in 100 words or fewer "Where In The World Your Love Will Come Alive," and mailing via first-class mail to: Silhouette 20ᵗʰ Anniversary Contest, (in the U.S.) P.O. Box 9069, Buffalo, NY 14269-9069; (In Canada) P.O. Box 637, Fort Erie, Ontario, Canada L2A 5X3. Limit one 8"x 11" mailed entry per person, household and e-mail address per day. On-line and/or 8"x 11" mailed entries received from persons residing in geographic areas in which Internet entry is not permissible will be disqualified. No liability is assumed for lost, late, incomplete, inaccurate, nondelivered or misdirected mail, or misdirected e-mail, for technical, hardware or software failures of any kind, lost or unavailable network connection, or failed, incomplete, garbled or delayed computer transmission or any human error which may occur in the receipt or processing of the entries in the contest.

3. Essays will be judged by a panel of members of the Silhouette editorial and marketing staff based on the following criteria:

   Sincerity (believability, credibility)—50%
   Originality (freshness, creativity)—30%
   Aptness (appropriateness to contest ideas)—20%

   Purchase or acceptance of a product offer does not improve your chances of winning. In the event of a tie, duplicate prizes will be awarded.

4. All entries become the property of Harlequin Enterprises Ltd., and will not be returned. Winner will be determined no later than 10/31/00 and will be notified by mail. Grand Prize winner will be required to sign and return Affidavit of Eligibility within 15 days of receipt of notification. Noncompliance within the time period may result in disqualification and an alternative winner may be selected. All municipal, provincial, federal, state and local laws and regulations apply. Contest open only to residents of the U.S. and Canada who are 18 years of age or older, and is void wherever prohibited by law. Internet entry is restricted solely to residents of those geographical areas in which Internet entry is permissible. Employees of Torstar Corp., their affiliates, agents and members of their immediate families are not eligible. Taxes on the prizes are the sole responsibility of winners. Entry and acceptance of any prize offered constitutes permission to use winner's name, photograph or other likeness for the purposes of advertising, trade and promotion on behalf of Torstar Corp. without further compensation to the winner, unless prohibited by law. Torstar Corp and D.L. Blair, Inc., their parents, affiliates and subsidiaries, are not responsible for errors in printing or electronic presentation of contest or entries. In the event of printing or other errors which may result in unintended prize values or duplication of prizes, all affected contest materials or entries shall be null and void. If for any reason the Internet portion of the contest is not capable of running as planned, including infection by computer virus, bugs, tampering, unauthorized intervention, fraud, technical failures, or any other causes beyond the control of Torstar Corp. which corrupt or affect the administration, secrecy, fairness, integrity or proper conduct of the contest, Torstar Corp. reserves the right, at its sole discretion, to disqualify any individual who tampers with the entry process and to cancel, terminate, modify or suspend the contest or the Internet portion thereof. In the event of a dispute regarding an on-line entry, the entry will be deemed submitted by the authorized holder of the e-mail account submitted at the time of entry. Authorized account holder is defined as the natural person who is assigned to an e-mail address by an Internet access provider, on-line service provider or other organization that is responsible for arranging e-mail address for the domain associated with the submitted e-mail address.

5. Prizes: Grand Prize—a $10,000 vacation to anywhere in the world. Travelers (at least one must be 18 years of age or older) or parent or guardian if one traveler is a minor, must sign and return a Release of Liability prior to departure. Travel must be completed by December 31, 2001, and is subject to space and accommodations availability. Two hundred (200) Second Prizes—a two-book limited edition autographed collector set from one of the Silhouette Anniversary authors: Nora Roberts, Diana Palmer, Linda Howard or Annette Broadrick (value $10.00 each set). All prizes are valued in U.S. dollars.

6. For a list of winners (available after 10/31/00), send a self-addressed, stamped envelope to: Harlequin Silhouette 20ᵗʰ Anniversary Winners, P.O. Box 4200, Blair, NE 68009-4200.

Contest sponsored by Torstar Corp., P.O. Box 9042, Buffalo, NY 14269-9042.

ENTER FOR A CHANCE TO WIN*

Silhouette's 20ᵗʰ Anniversary Contest

Tell Us Where in the World You Would Like *Your* Love To Come Alive... And We'll Send the Lucky Winner There!

Silhouette wants to take you wherever your happy ending can come true.

Here's how to enter: Tell us, in 100 words or less, where you want to go to make your love come alive!

In addition to the grand prize, there will be 200 runner-up prizes, collector's-edition book sets autographed by one of the Silhouette anniversary authors: **Nora Roberts, Diana Palmer, Linda Howard** or **Annette Broadrick.**

DON'T MISS YOUR CHANCE TO WIN! ENTER NOW! No Purchase Necessary

Silhouette®

Where love comes alive™

Name:

Address:

City: State/Province:

Zip/Postal Code:

Mail to Harlequin Books: **In the U.S.:** P.O. Box 9069, Buffalo, NY 14269-9069; **In Canada:** P.O. Box 637, Fort Erie, Ontario, L4A 5X3

*No purchase necessary—for contest details send a self-addressed stamped envelope to: Silhouette's 20ᵗʰ Anniversary Contest, P.O. Box 9069, Buffalo, NY, 14269-9069 (include contest name on self-addressed envelope). Residents of Washington and Vermont may omit postage. Open to Cdn. (excluding Quebec) and U.S. residents who are 18 or over. Void where prohibited. Contest ends August 31, 2000.

PS20CON_R